THE MAGIC FARAWAY TREE

A CHRISTMAS ADVENTURE

Also by Jacqueline Wilson:

The Magic Faraway Tree: A New Adventure

Look out for these other
Magic Faraway Tree stories by

Enid Blyton

The Enchanted Wood
The Magic Faraway Tree
The Folk of the Faraway Tree
Adventure of the Goblin Dog

Picture books:

The Magic Faraway Tree: Silky's Story
The Magic Faraway Tree: Moonface's Story

THE MAGIC FARAWAY TREE

A CHRISTMAS ADVENTURE

Illustrated by
MARK BEECH

Inspired by
Enid Blyton

JACQUELINE WILSON

Hodder

HODDER CHILDREN'S BOOKS
First published in Great Britain in 2023 by
Hodder & Stoughton Limited

1 3 5 7 9 10 8 6 4 2

A CIP catalogue record for this book is available from the British Library.

Hardback: 978 1 444 97154 5
WTS edition: 978 1 444 97547 5

Paperback: 978 1 444 97158 3
Trade Paperback: 978 1 444 97157 6

Typeset in Caslon Twelve by Avon DataSet Ltd, Alcester, Warwickshire

Printed and bound in Great Britain by Clays Ltd, Elcograf S.p.A.

The paper and board used in this book are
made from wood from responsible sources.

MIX
Paper from
responsible sources
FSC® C104740

Hodder Children's Books
An imprint of Hachette Children's Group
Part of Hodder & Stoughton Limited
Carmelite House
50 Victoria Embankment
London EC4Y 0DZ

An Hachette UK Company
www.hachette.co.uk
www.hachettechildrens.co.uk

To Gary Freemantle
The best technical wizard in the world
With many thanks

CHAPTER
ONE

'WE WISH you a merry Christmas!' Milo sang.

'We *wish* you a merry *Christmas*!' Mia sang.

'We wish you a merry Christmas!' Birdy sang at the top of her voice.

'And a happy New Year!' they sang together, and then they started all over again.

'Please! No more! That's the tenth time!' Mum protested.

'How am I supposed to concentrate on my driving with you lot bellowing Christmas carols?' Dad said.

Their parents weren't really cross though. Everyone was in a happy holiday mood.

'Just one more time!' Birdy begged.

Mum and Dad joined in *several* more times before they saw the sign to the motorway services and turned off to park there. It took a while to find a space because so many people were travelling to spend Christmas with their family or friends. When they climbed out of the car, at last, they heard familiar music.

'We wish you a merry Christmas!' A group of carol singers were standing outside the entrance in woollen hats and thick coats, singing away.

'Let's go and sing with them!' said Birdy.

'We can't do that, silly!' said Milo.

'People would think we were showing off,' said Mia, tutting at their little sister.

'I *like* showing off!' said Birdy, and she ran to join the carol singers before they could stop her.

She smiled at them and joined in the chorus, singing heartily. Birdy wasn't worried when they started singing the verse. She didn't know the words, but she just went la-la-la, more or less keeping in tune. The carol singers didn't seem to

A CHRISTMAS ADVENTURE

mind. They were all looking at her, smiling. Other people were smiling too, and saying she was sweet, and a little pet.

'Mum, Dad, *stop* her!' said Milo, going red.

'She's hopeless!' said Mia, rolling her eyes.

'But she *is* sweet and nobody seems to mind,' said Dad. He always said he didn't have any favourites – but if he *did* they were sure it would be Birdy.

'Still, I think she's had her little moment,' said Mum. She went over and took hold of Birdy's hand. 'Come on, pet.'

Birdy smiled at everyone and waved her free hand. They all went, 'Aaaah!'

Milo and Mia sighed. They loved their younger sister, but she could be a royal pain at times.

They were playing more Christmas songs inside the cafe. Birdy started to sing along again, but Mum shook her head.

'I think that's enough now,' she said. 'Come on, what do we all want to eat? I'm going to have one of those rainbow salads.'

'Well, I'm going to have fish and chips,' said Dad.

'Fried chicken, chicken, chicken!' said Milo.

'I'd like a veggie burger please,' said Mia.

'I'd like a doughnut!' said Birdy.

It took quite a while to gather all their choices from the different outlets. Mum said Birdy had to eat something with protein, so she peeled the top piece of bread off an egg mayonnaise sandwich and nibbled at it before she was allowed the doughnut. She ended up with egg mixture in her ears and jam all down her chin and needed a thorough wash in the Ladies' room afterwards.

Then they all went to the sweet shop to choose special treats for Christmas. Mum and Dad wanted a big tin of chocolate toffees because everyone liked them. They said Milo and Mia and Birdy could each choose one chocolate bar for themselves. They wandered around together, trying to make up their minds.

'Look!' said Milo, pointing to a big multipack of ten different kinds of chocolate. 'It says, "We Wish You a Merry Christmas!"'

Birdy immediately started singing again.

'Stop it!' said Mia, giving her a little nudge. 'Hey, we'd get three bars each, plus one over!'

'And I'd get the extra one because I spotted the packet and I'm the oldest,' said Milo.

'No, I'd get *all* of them because I'm the youngest,' said Birdy. She couldn't do division yet, but she was very good at arguing.

'Perhaps we ought to give a chocolate bar each to Mum and Dad, because our Christmas presents to them aren't all that great,' said Mia.

She had made cross-stitch coin purses for both of them. She'd worked hard, but trying to stitch neatly had made *her* very cross. Milo had made Mum and Dad a bookmark each out of leather. He'd written their names with a special gold pen, but they'd gone a bit smudgy. Birdy had made 'books' for both her parents. She'd cut out pieces of paper with her special blunt scissors and Mia had sewn them together for her to make two little booklets. Birdy had drawn a picture of Mum on one and a picture of Dad on the other. They looked identical – two circles with dots for eyes and smiley mouths, and little stick arms and legs.

'Mum and Dad say they *like* homemade presents,' said Milo, but he could see Mia had a point.

'I made my lovely books for Mum and Dad,' said Birdy. 'I want to give a chocolate bar to Silky for her Christmas present.'

'Oh, no! We haven't got proper Christmas presents for all our Faraway Tree friends!' said Milo.

'We have to give Silky a present – and Moonface. And Pippin!' said Mia.

They were going to spend Christmas at the same holiday cottage they'd stayed in during the summer. It was on the edge of the wonderful Enchanted Wood. They had spent almost every day of their summer holiday in the middle of the woods, climbing up the amazing Faraway Tree and making friends with all the folk who lived there.

Silky was a kind fairy whose wings changed colour to match her beautiful dresses. Milo and Mia had thought they were long past the age of believing in fairies, but they had to agree that Silky was real.

Her best friend was Moonface, a sweet-natured magical man who could cast spells – sometimes! Pippin was an adorable talking bear cub who now had his own little bear cave in the Faraway Tree.

'Then what about the Saucepan Man and Mr Watzisname? They're our friends too,' said Milo.

'And Dame Washalot,' said Mia.

'Yes, she's a friend, though she's a menace when she empties her washtub down the tree and we get soaked,' said Milo.

'Especially you,' said Birdy, giggling.

'The Angry Pixie pours his jug of water over you too,' Mia pointed out.

'Well, maybe he'll stop doing it if we give him a Christmas present,' said Milo.

'He'll be a Happy Pixie then,' said Mia.

'So how many chocolate bars is that?' Milo wondered, counting on his fingers. 'Seven! So we still get one each! Awesome!'

'Yay! Awesome!' echoed Birdy. 'Can Silky have the biggest one?'

'Pippin must have the honeycomb bar!' said Mia.

'And we must give Moonface the big chocolate toffee bar because he loves toffee so,' said Milo, who was a big fan of Moonface's special Toffee Shocks.

'I can't wait to see them all!' said Mia.

Mum and Dad were happy to buy their multipack choice for them. They didn't explain it was going to be a present. Mum and Dad didn't know anything about their magic friends in the Faraway Tree. They'd just never believe it was possible to chat to a fairy or have tea with a little man who looked like the moon. Even Birdy knew she must never ever tell their parents just in case it would break some spell and they'd never find their way to the Faraway Tree ever again.

There was a toy vending machine near the exit to the car park – the sort where you work a special crane to grab one of the colourful teddies crammed inside. Dad was in such a jolly mood, he dug out some change from his pocket.

'Oh, dear, it's all in a muddle,' said Dad. 'I wish I had a special coin purse to keep it safe.'

'Really?' said Mia joyfully. She had the first go

on the machine, but couldn't manage to hook a toy, though several times she grazed an ear or a paw.

'Let me have a go. You're rubbish!' said Milo.

Milo found he wasn't any better and got annoyed. Birdy had her go and actually managed to lift a plump fairy up by her wings, but she couldn't make the crane keep hold of her. She got upset too, because she wanted it so much.

'Hey, kids, cheer up,' said Dad. 'No one's allowed to be grumpy when it's nearly Christmas! *I'll* have a go.'

He had several tries, but with no success whatsoever.

'It's a fix!' he said. 'There's no way anyone could get one of those wretched toys out – they're too tightly jammed in.'

'Now who's getting grumpy?' said Mum. 'Shall I have a go?'

She had three tries and manipulated the crane with such steady precision that she captured three toys. Each time, she slowly and carefully kept the claws of the crane clasped as she swung it over and dropped it down the chute. Mum seized the plump fairy for Birdy, a green toy unicorn for Mia and a scarlet dragon for Milo.

They all cheered Mum – and Dad had the grace to cheer her loudest of all. Then they set off in the car again, and sang some more Christmas songs, and after a while the children got sleepy. It was rather a squash in the back, especially as Birdy had insisted on taking Gilbert, her huge toy dog, on holiday too. He was almost as big as she was.

Milo was shunted right up against one side of the back seat and Mia the other, and Birdy could hardly breathe with hairy Gilbert sprawled all over her, but at last they stopped fidgeting and fell fast asleep.

They didn't wake up until Dad called out, 'We're nearly there, kids!'

They peered out of the windows into the grey dusk and could just make out a vast wood down the hill below them, with one very tall tree that reached all the way up to the gathering clouds. The Magic Faraway Tree!

CHAPTER TWO

DAD PARKED the car outside the holiday cottage and the children tumbled out and went running up to the door. It didn't look quite the same in the winter, without hollyhocks and cornflowers and poppies in the front garden, and roses and honeysuckle growing around the porch.

'We'll make a Christmas wreath and hang it on the door,' said Mum. 'We can gather little branches and twigs and see if we can find any holly and mistletoe in the wood. Come and help unload the car now.'

There were lots of big bags and suitcases and a

hamper of food. They helped lug everything to the door, and then Dad fumbled with the key. He had to rub his hands hard because they were cramped from holding the steering wheel and it was very cold. They'd had the heater on in the car and now it was nearly night-time it was a shock to discover it was freezing, with an icy wind.

'Is it cold enough for snow?' Milo asked hopefully, wrapping his arms round himself.

'It will look so fantastic for Christmas, everything crisp and white and beautiful,' said Mia, jumping up and down.

'We wish you a merry Christmas!' Birdy muttered, clutching Gilbert for warmth.

Dad got the door open at last and they rushed inside the cottage and snapped on the light. It was just as cold inside the cottage as outside, maybe even colder.

'Don't worry – we'll get the boiler lit and the radiators will heat up in no time,' said Mum.

'We'll be as warm as toast in five minutes,' said Dad, picking Birdy up and swinging her round and round.

It didn't take five minutes. It didn't take fifteen. It didn't take fifty. Dad moved over for Mum to have a go. Then Dad tried again, and gingerly took the front part off the boiler to have had a good peer, using his phone as a torch. They had to admit defeat. The boiler was broken.

'Never mind, we'll have a proper fire in the living room. There are lots of logs in the woodpile outside. It'll be really cosy,' said Dad, while Mum was phoning the holiday letting company.

The children kept their coats on and helped Dad build up a log fire in the living room grate. It took him a very long time to get the fire going. The children huddled around, teeth chattering. It didn't feel very Christmassy at all, though no one liked to say so.

'I know!' said Milo. 'Mia and Birdy and I will go out the back and run up and down the lane to get warm!'

'Oh, yes!' said Mia.

'Awesome!' said Birdy, which was her new favourite word.

They knew Milo didn't really mean they should run races. He was suggesting they jump over the ditch that separated the lane from the Enchanted Wood, and make their way to the Faraway Tree in the dark! They could meet all their friends and warm up in Silky's bright little house while she made them flying pancakes. Or they could climb up to Moonface's round room, fill their mouths with a Toffee Shock and whizz down the slippery-slip that led from the middle of his floor down through the trunk of the Faraway Tree to the ground.

'You're not going out in the pitch-dark,' said Mum. 'Don't be daft!'

'We'll take the blankets off the beds and huddle up here,' said Dad. 'We could play bears!'

Milo wrinkled up his nose in an expression that clearly meant *pathetic*.

'Oh, Dad, we're not little kids!' said Mia.

Birdy *was* a little kid and would have loved a game of bears with Dad, but it would never be the same as going to the Magic Faraway Tree and playing with a *real* bear. Dad was looking hurt and she wished she could explain, but knew it was impossible.

She climbed on Dad's lap instead and put her arms round him.

'This is a bear hug,' she said, and made Dad smile.

In the end they had a good supper of sausages and bacon and baked beans and tomatoes, all cooked on the small electric stove, and then they played board games.

'I'm *bored* of playing board games,' Milo whispered to Mia, wishing the cottage had broadband, or at the very least a television, but he cheered up when he won Ludo.

Then Dad read them a story with some very funny rude bits, which made them all laugh, and Mum read them a story about a girl who was very naughty and played dares, which made them all gasp. Then they took turns reading their favourite story about a magic land where there were fairies and amazing creatures and animals who could talk. It made them all sigh.

'This is a great story, Dad,' said Milo.

'We love it,' said Mia.

'It's awesome,' said Birdy. 'It just makes us want to—'

'Birdy!' said Milo and Mia simultaneously.

'I was only going to say it makes us want to go *there*,' said Birdy.

It was so hard to know that their own magic world was only a hop and step away from the back door, but they could hear the wind howling outside, and rain had started pattering against the little latticed windows. They knew there was no point trying to make Mum and Dad relent and let them outside.

They went up to bed early because they were all hoping they might get a glimpse of Silky flying past their cottage. Birdy had spotted her the first night at the cottage in the summer holidays. Milo and Mia were ashamed to admit that they hadn't believed her at first. But now they crowded into Birdy's small attic room and peered out of the window hopefully.

The rain was really lashing down now, and the

wind rattled the windowpane unnervingly. They waited and waited, shivering in their pyjamas, with their outdoor coats on top. Mia even made Birdy put on her woolly hat and mittens, because she was worried about her catching cold.

'If it's so cold for us in here, then Silky's hardly likely to be flying around in the midst of this storm,' said Milo.

'I think Milo's right, Birdy,' said Mia sadly. 'It's freezing. Let's just go to bed. We'll see her tomorrow!'

'I need to see her now!' said Birdy. 'She always comes when I'm here!'

'Yes, but she doesn't know you're here, does she?' said Mia.

'I wrote her a letter saying we were coming for Christmas!' Birdy insisted.

She'd certainly written what she said was a letter. They'd seen Birdy laboriously scribbling line after line on a page of her drawing book. They were very wobbly lines and her spelling was questionable. She'd signed it 'Luv from Birdy' and drawn a little blob with a beak and sticky-out wings and two tiny legs. Then she'd ripped the page out of her book and wrapped it up in an old envelope she'd found in the wastepaper basket.

Birdy had remembered that envelopes had to have an address, so she'd printed 'Silky the Fary, The Farwy Tree' on it and then popped it in the Christmas card post box at school.

She was disappointed not to get a reply the very next day. She became fretful the day after. Mia had comforted Birdy by saying that maybe Silky couldn't read and write properly as she hadn't been to school. 'But I'm sure she got someone to read your letter to her. She'd have been thrilled,' Mia had said.

Mia sighed, realising Birdy had believed her. Milo was yawning and thumping his arms to try to get the blood circulating.

'I don't think I've ever been so cold in my life!' he complained. 'Sorry, Birdy, but we've got to go to bed now or we'll all turn into snowmen.'

'You two can go to bed. *I'm* staying up to see Silky,' said Birdy determinedly. 'Oh, I think she's coming right now!'

'You're making it up, Birdy,' said Mia.

'No, I'm not! I can see her, look!' Birdy insisted, jumping up and down.

'It's pitch-black outside,' said Milo, yawning again – but Mia suddenly clutched him.

'Look!' she repeated, transfixed.

There was a small silvery light in the distance, like a tiny moon. It was getting nearer and nearer – and soon they could make out the distinctive winged shape of a little flying creature. It wasn't a bird, it wasn't a bat – it was a fairy. Not just any old fairy.

It was Silky!

She was wearing a silver raincoat and she had a matching silver hat on her head and silver boots on her delicately pointed feet. She'd grown large, powerful silver wings that gleamed in the rain and steadied her in the wind. She was flying straight towards them, a beaming smile on her lovely face.

'Silky!' they all breathed.

She came right up to the round attic window and put her hand on the glass. Birdy stretched up and put her hand on it too. Milo and Mia put their hands either side of hers. They all smiled back at

Silky and mouthed hello.

'See you tomorrow?' she said.

They couldn't hear through the glass, especially with the noise of the wind and the rain, but they all made out her words. They nodded vigorously and mouthed, '*Yes!*'

Silky turned herself round gracefully, bobbing in the air, and took something out of her raincoat pocket. It was Birdy's letter.

'*Thank you!*' she mouthed, and then flew away.

CHAPTER THREE

MILO, MIA and Birdy all woke up at the same time. They listened. The wind was still howling. The rain was slapping at the window. It was very, very cold. So very cold that it was awful getting out of bed, but they had to run to the window to see if it had somehow snowed in the night.

It was still pitch-dark outside – but they could tell there was no wonderful white covering of snow anywhere.

'Perhaps it will snow later on,' said Mum when they trailed downstairs, disappointed. She was fully dressed in her jumper and jeans and wearing her cosy dressing gown over the top.

'Never mind, we'll go out later and have lunch in front of a roaring fire in a pub,' said Dad. He was wearing *all* his jumpers, one over the other, and a beanie hat pulled down to his eyebrows.

'We have to wait in for the plumber to come first,' said Mum. 'I do hope he can fix the wretched boiler. I wish I'd brought some porridge oats. We need something hot to warm us up.'

'Never mind, Mum, we'll warm ourselves up,' said Mia, taking Birdy's hands. They jumped up and down together until they were breathless.

'And we could run races in the lane outside after breakfast,' said Milo.

'Oh, yes!' said Mia and Birdy.

'Oh, no!' said Mum. 'It's much too dark and windy and wet to play outside.'

'We'll wear our wellies,' said Mia. 'And put heaps of clothes on.'

'We simply *have* to go to the lane!' said Birdy. 'Because we have a special secret!'

'Birdy! Sh! Shut *up*!' said Milo and Mia, thinking

she was about to tell Mum and Dad about the Magic Faraway Tree!

'There's no need to go shush at me and tell me to shut up!' Birdy said indignantly. 'I was just going to say that our special secret is that I'm getting better and better at running and I can nearly beat Mia and Milo, so I'm almost the champion, aren't I?'

'Oh,' said Milo limply. 'Yes, I suppose so.'

'Yay, Birdy the champion,' said Mia, without enthusiasm.

Birdy smiled smugly. 'So I have to practise, don't I, Dad?'

'If you're very careful, sweetheart,' said Dad.

The three children golloped their breakfast and then rushed to put on yet more clothes to go outside.

'Aren't I clever?' Birdy kept saying, in an insufferable way, but Milo and Mia put up with it because she really *had* been clever, and Mum and Dad might not have relented otherwise.

Birdy had maybe been a little *too* clever, because Dad insisted on coming out to the lane to watch her running. She was actually even slower than usual because she was wearing her jeans *and* her dungarees and her duffle coat over her dressing gown and could barely move – but Dad still cheered her on. But then luckily Mum called to say the plumber's van was drawing up outside the front door, so Dad went back inside to talk to him.

Milo and Mia and Birdy quickly held hands and with one hop, skip and a jump they cleared the little ditch and were in the Enchanted Wood. The trees waved their bare branches in the wind, and the rain poured down relentlessly.

'Why aren't the trees making their *wisha-wisha-wisha* sound?' asked Birdy.

'They haven't got any leaves because it's winter,' said Milo.

'It all looks so different now,' said Mia. 'It doesn't seem quite as friendly as it was in the summer.'

'Well, it should be easy-peasy to find our way to the Faraway Tree now,' said Milo.

It wasn't as easy as he'd thought. They tried one path, then another.

'It must be *this* one,' said Mia, but after striding

around for ten minutes they found themselves back at the edge of the wood.

'This doesn't make sense,' said Milo.

'We need one of the animals to help us,' said Mia.

But there were no rabbits, no squirrels, no deer in sight.

'They're all sheltering from the weather,' said Mia, peering up to see if she could spot any birds. The rain poured down on her face, making her blink.

'I wish Silky would come and show us the way,' said Birdy. She started calling her. 'Silky! Silky! *Silky!*'

A solitary crow flew up in the air, squawking at her angrily. Birdy jumped, frightened. She was shivering so much that Milo and Mia got worried.

'Maybe we ought to take her home to get her dry?' Milo muttered to Mia.

'And get us dry too,' said Mia, whose winter coat wasn't waterproof. She was wet right through to her underwear and squelched as she walked.

'No, we have to find the Faraway Tree!' Birdy

insisted, with chattering teeth. 'SILKY! SILKY! SILKY!' Then she gave a great shriek and pointed.

There was a glint of silver in the distance. It was flying towards them, circling the trees, getting nearer and nearer.

'It *is* Silky!' they cried together.

She landed neatly in front of them, still dainty in spite of her big silver boots.

Silky hugged them all, and they hugged her back damply, as the rain poured down.

'I'm so sorry I'm late!' she said. 'Poor Pippin got a little bit burnt and I had to rub my special soothing lotion all over his furry face.'

'He got burnt? Is the Land of Dragons back?' Milo asked eagerly.

'No, it's a much more delightful land! I won't tell you what it is – I want it to be a lovely surprise,' said Silky. 'I promise you'll like it there.'

'Is Pippin all right now?' Mia asked.

'He's fine, don't worry,' said Silky. 'He's longing to meet you. He wanted to come with me, but he can't fly, so I knew I'd be quicker on my own. Follow me, my dear friends!' Silky spread her umbrella wings again.

She flew up in the air and the children held hands and stumbled after her. They went down one of the little paths and this time reached the Magic Faraway Tree in a matter of moments.

'We're here!' said Mia, stretching her arms wide to give the tree a hug.

'Mind out, Mia, you're standing by the exit of the slippery-slip. Someone might come bursting out of the trapdoor on their cushion and knock you flying!' said Milo. 'Oh, I can't wait to have a go myself!'

'I think you'll have to wait a bit. Moonface is having a little holiday up in the magic land,' said Silky. 'We all are!'

'Is it raining there?' asked Mia.

Silky shook her head happily. 'Come and see!'

They started climbing the tree. It didn't seem to be bearing any fruit now. Holly and mistletoe grew on the branches, but they didn't look very Christmassy in the pouring rain. They passed the

Angry Pixie's window, but he didn't peer out and throw a jug of water over them. They passed Silky's yellow front door. The children rather hoped she'd invite them in and offer them towels to get dry and give them one of her delicious snacks.

'You'll get dry soon enough in the magic land,' Silky said, seeming to guess what they were thinking. 'And there are wonderful refreshments!'

They went past Moonface's house. He'd nailed a message to his front door that said, 'On holiday, hurray!'

Dame Washalot was on holiday too, her washtub empty, with no clothes flapping on her washing line. Pippin wasn't in his bear cave, though his little recycling bin was brimming over with empty honey pots, which made the children laugh fondly. The Saucepan Man and Mr Watzisname weren't home either and had obviously gone up to the mystery magic land above their heads too.

'Whatever can this land be?' said Milo, as they stopped climbing for a few seconds to catch their breath. He tried not to look down. Because the

Magic Faraway Tree didn't have leaves now, he could see all the way through the branches to the ground far, far below. Milo never wanted to admit it, but he was really scared of heights. 'Do you think the Land of Bouncy Castles has come back? Everyone went to that to have fun, didn't they?'

'Well, if it is, we're all so wrapped up we'll bounce up and down like beach balls,' said Mia.

'I think it's the Land of Christmas!' said Birdy. 'And there'll be snow and presents and Santa Claus will be there going, "Ho, ho, ho."'

'Oh, Birdy, I think you're right!' said Milo.

'I do hope so!' said Mia. 'And if Santa is here, maybe his reindeer will be too! I'd just love to see eight reindeer.'

'Santa has nine reindeer, if you count Rudolph,' said Milo.

'No, it's eight, because otherwise they wouldn't be able to pull the sleigh evenly,' said Mia.

They had a pointless argument about it as they started climbing again, while Birdy scrambled up fast and got to the golden ladder at the top of the tree first. Silky was perching on the rungs, smiling all over her face.

'Well done!' she said. 'Are you feeling a bit warmer now?'

Birdy realised she *was* much warmer. She'd stopped shivering. The tip of her nose was no longer frozen. In fact she felt positively hot. She took off her woolly hat and shook her hair, blowing upwards to cool her face. 'I'm boiling!' she said. 'I'm going to take my coat off. And my dressing gown!'

'I should leave everything on just until you get up the ladder. There are special lockers up there where we can safely store our clothes,' said Silky. She reached out her hand and pulled Birdy up beside her.

Birdy scampered up the ladder and poked her head out of the clouds. Mia and Milo heard her give a great whoop of excitement.

'It *must* be the Land of Christmas!' said Mia.

'So why is it starting to feel so warm?' Milo asked.

They found out when they got to the top of the ladder. It wasn't the Land of Christmas at all. It was the Land of Sunshine!

The sun was a great golden globe right above them. There wasn't a cloud in the cornflower-blue sky, and the nearby sea sparkled in the sunshine. They stared, unable to believe the contrast in the weather.

'It's so fantastic!' said Milo.

'Amazing!' said Mia.

'Awesome!' said Birdy.

A cheery elf in a dazzling white uniform nodded at them. He wore a peaked sailor's cap on his head. His long, pointy ears kept it neatly in place. He had long, pointy feet too, clad in special, long, pointy deck shoes. He clicked his heels together and saluted them.

'It is always fantastic, amazing and awesome in the Land of Sunshine, my dears,' he said, grinning. 'Please come and select your summer clothes and I will show you where to get changed.'

The elf led them inside a big white building that contained everything anyone could possibly want for a perfect summer holiday. There were shorts and T-shirts and sandals and flip-flops and a huge variety of sunhats and baseball caps. Buckets and spades and beach balls. Swimming costumes, some large and enveloping, some tiny bikinis, and beach robes and the fluffiest towels. Sun lotion and sunglasses and shelf after shelf of paperbacks and magazines. Popcorn and sweets and crisps and fruit. Cold cabinets with an array of fizzy drinks and juices. And a giant freezer of ice cream and ice lollies and a machine making all different flavours of Whippy ices – vanilla, chocolate, strawberry, salted caramel, blackcurrant and raspberry ripple.

'At your service, madam, children,' said at least ten white-uniformed elves to Silky and Milo and Mia and Birdy.

They were so boiling hot in their winter clothes that they took off all their many coats and hats and gloves and scarves and had an ice cream first of all. Silky chose a yellow mango lolly studded all over with raspberries, Milo had the hugest chocolate cone ever with a whirl of cream on top, Mia had a big white ice cream on a stick in the shape of a polar bear and Birdy hopped around for ages unable to decide, and eventually chose a Whippy made of every single flavour with strawberry sauce and two chocolate flakes.

When they were finished another elf brought the children much-needed face flannels and towels (Silky managed to eat her mango lolly without getting a single drip on her silver dress) and then they chose their summer clothes. That was easy enough. Milo picked red swimming shorts with a navy T-shirt with a great gold star on the front. Mia chose a sky-blue swimming costume, with a blue T-shirt and shorts to match. Her T-shirt said 'Champion' in red letters. Birdy badly wanted to wear a mermaid costume, which was very beautiful, but they pointed out that she wouldn't be able to walk anywhere wearing the shimmering mermaid tail, let alone run on the sand or paddle, so she reluctantly chose a red swimming costume with a red sun suit patterned with white seagulls to wear on top.

Silky didn't need to choose clothes off the rail. She simply concentrated hard and changed her dress to a pearly pink silk over a white swimming costume, while her wings changed from silver to a dazzling white. The children stored their winter clothes in handy lockers, marvelling that they could have worn so many woolly layers.

'Have a lovely day at the beach,' said the elves.

The first elf with the peaked cap added, 'Let's hope it stays sunny for you!'

All the other elves collapsed with laughter. The children blinked at them, bewildered.

'It's *always* sunny in the Land of Sunshine,' said Silky. 'Would you like another ice cream to eat on the way to the beach?'

'You bet!' said Milo.

'Awesome!' said Birdy.

'Another?' said Mia, hesitating. Mum and Dad would never ever let them have another ice cream ten minutes after the first one.

Silky smiled. 'You can eat ice creams all day long if you like. Everyone stays fit and healthy and happy in the Land of Sunshine.'

'Then I wish we could stay here for ever!' said Mia, choosing an orange-striped lolly in the shape of a tiger. It had lime-flavoured ice cream inside, deliciously sharp.

Milo selected an animal ice lolly too, in the shape of an elephant. It was enormous, with white coconut tusks and banana-flavoured ice cream inside.

Birdy was delighted to find a turquoise dog-shaped ice lolly that was the spitting image of Gilbert. He had strawberry ice cream inside.

'If only Gilbert had strawberry ice cream inside him!' said Birdy.

'But then you'd eat him all up,' said Mia.

'I'd only lick him a few times each day, so he'd last a very long time,' said Birdy.

'But you'd have to keep him ice-cold or he'd melt everywhere,' said Milo indistinctly, his mouth full of elephant lolly.

'And he wouldn't fit in the fridge in the cottage – he's much too big,' said Mia.

'It's so cold there he wouldn't *need* to be in the fridge,' Birdy argued.

'You children make me laugh,' said Silky, delicately licking a raspberry-flavoured Whippy

with a real raspberry topping and a little whirl of cream. 'You're always squabbling, and yet it's just in fun.'

'Don't you have brothers and sisters, Silky?' asked Mia.

'Oh, yes,' said Silky. 'But I don't get to see them very often since I moved to the Magic Faraway Tree. They still live in the Land of Fairies.'

'Oh, I would absolutely love to go to the Land of Fairies!' said Birdy.

Mia and Milo weren't quite so sure. They loved Silky and were proud to be her friend, but they weren't sure they wanted to go to a land *full* of fairies. What if they had to dress up as fairies themselves? The thought of wearing flouncy dresses with matching wings was alarming.

'The Land of Fairies hardly ever comes to the top of the Magic Faraway Tree,' said Silky, but she was smiling. 'However, I think I might get to see my family before too long. And the Land of Sunshine is one of my special favourite lands because it's so happy.'

She led them along the beautiful pink esplanade beside the glittering sea to the steps that led down to the white sands. The children stood there a moment, shading their eyes, and spotted all their Faraway Tree friends. There was Moonface, looking splendid in a big, flowery short-sleeved shirt and scarlet shorts that showed off his spindly white legs. He was paddling in the shallows, holding hands with two baby squirrels who were jumping up and down excitedly and splashing with their bushy tails. A long line of squirrels frolicked with them, all splashing too, though the oldest squirrel, Mr Red, was doing his best to keep them in order.

Dame Washalot and her friend Dame Ironallday were paddling too, their long dresses tucked into their bloomers. They were wearing jolly sunhats with 'Kiss Me Quick' on the front, and were jumping up and down like schoolgirls, squealing with laughter. The Saucepan Man and Mr Watzisname were watching them from special red-and-yellow-striped beach loungers, sipping drinks through straws. The Saucepan Man looked very skinny without his saucepans and wearing a long navy swimsuit. He wore just one saucepan as a sunhat. Mr Watzisname wore a matching swimsuit, and looked stouter than usual because he had put a blow-up rubber lifebelt round his large waist. It fitted so snugly, he couldn't pull it off. The Angry Pixie had joined them, sprawled on his own sun-lounger, barely recognisable in rainbow shorts, with a great contented grin on his face. He had a jug of liquid by his side – but it was simply to replenish his own fruity drink.

There was Pippin, wearing a straw sunhat and a white T-shirt, gambolling over the sands to give them a big bear hug each, still a little sticky from his soothing sun cream – and the pot of honey he was clutching in his paw.

The children hugged him back, so happy to see him again, and then ran with him along the sands. Mia looked far out across the sea, shading her eyes, peering intently. Then she stopped still.

'Look!' she cried out, pointing. 'Look, look, look!'

CHAPTER
FOUR

THEY ALL stared out to sea. The distant waves had white tips. But when Milo and Birdy rubbed their eyes and stared harder they saw why Mia was pointing so dramatically. Sea unicorns! Not just one. Many of them, one to each wave, rearing up magnificently with their long white manes flowing and their horns glinting in the sunlight.

'Oh!' Mia cried, tearing off her new shorts and kicking off her flip-flops. She started running hard across the sands.

'No, Mia! Come back!' Milo called after her. 'They're much too far away! You'll never be able to swim that far!'

Mia didn't hear him. She didn't hear Birdy yelling. She didn't hear Pippin giving little high-pitched growls.

'Stop her, Silky! Please, fly after her!' Milo begged.

But Silky didn't even look worried. 'It's all right, I promise you. Nothing bad can ever happen in the Land of Sunshine. Mia will be fine,' she said serenely.

'How can she possibly be fine? She's quite a good swimmer, almost as good as me, but I couldn't swim that far, not when the sea's quite rough out there,' Milo shouted. 'But I suppose I'll have to go after her, seeing as she's my sister.' He started ripping undone the laces of his brand-new white trainers, hopping on one leg.

'No, Milo, you don't have to do that! Look again,' said Silky.

Milo looked. Birdy peered. They saw one of the sea unicorns riding a huge wave almost as tall as the Faraway Tree. He shone with the iridescent colours of the sea, all shades of blue and green and purple, and his long mane flew out in a white froth. The wave was rolling rapidly towards Mia, who was in the sea now and swimming as fast as she could.

'It'll swamp her! She'll drown!' Milo shouted, running across the sand, with Birdy staggering after him, shrieking.

But as the enormous wave powered to the shallows it suddenly subsided, though ripples spread far across the sea, and Moonface and Dame Washalot and Dame Ironallday and all the little squirrels got splashed. The sea unicorn swam on towards Mia and she swam towards him. He bent his head and Mia reached up and threw her arms joyfully round his great neck.

'It's you! It's you, my lovely, lovely unicorn!' she cried, pulling herself up on to his shining back.

'Is she all right now?' Birdy asked anxiously, tugging at Milo.

'I don't know!' he said. 'What if he carries her away across the sea?'

'He won't. They'll just enjoy their special reunion and then he'll bring Mia to the shallows and swim back out to his brothers,' said Silky.

'How can you be so sure? You were so worried when he carried her away last time,' Milo protested, one shoe off and one shoe on.

'That was in the Land of Unicorns, where anything can happen. I keep telling you, this is the Land of Sunshine,' said Silky.

Milo squinted into the sunlight and focused on his sister. She had her head back in delight, her hair flying in the wind. He had never seen her look so happy. She reached forward and stroked the sea unicorn's shining head. It could have been an illusion of the light, but he seemed to be smiling. The sea unicorn turned and took her further out, pausing and treading water, and then swooped back towards the shore. Milo heard Mia's faint scream of joy.

'She's happy, Milo,' said Birdy, taking hold of his hand. 'Come and paddle with me!'

'You're right, Birdy. You and Silky. I can see she's happy,' said Milo. He usually hated admitting he was wrong, but now he didn't really mind at all. Perhaps it was because he felt happy too.

Milo gave Birdy a piggyback across the sands, and she laughed, clasping the hair on his head and patting him as if he were a unicorn too. Silky flew over their heads and he did his best to race her to the shallows. He knew he didn't have any chance of winning because Birdy was surprisingly heavy for a small girl and Silky was a fairy with powerful wings, but somehow he beat her by a few seconds. Perhaps Silky had flown extra leisurely on purpose.

Birdy leapt off Milo's back and went splashing through the turquoise water to greet Moonface, not even bothering to kick off her flip-flops first. Milo took time to take off his box-fresh trainers and stored them neatly on the sand, folded his socks on top, and then ran into the water himself. It was deliciously cold on his hot toes, but when he plunged in to swim the water was lukewarm and wonderful. He waved to Moonface and the two dames and all the squirrels and the Saucepan Man and Mr Watzisname and the Angry Pixie on their loungers and then dived down into the water. He touched the sand and shells at the bottom, and then burst up again, spouting water.

Milo had fun larking around pretending to be a dolphin, even making little squeaking noises, *eek-eek-eek*. There seemed to be an echo underwater, because he heard more eeks all around him. Milo thrust his head out of the water again and seemed to see three plump heads bobbing around him, with strange snouts, little beady eyes and huge, smiley mouths. Milo blinked his eyes clear of seawater to have a proper look.

'Real dolphins!' he gasped.

They laughed in a friendly fashion, and then, taking it in turns, dived down into the water and up

again in a perfect arc. Milo clapped each one. Then they nodded at him and *eek-eek-eeked* encouragingly.

'OK, I'll have a go, but I'll be rubbish compared to you guys,' he said. He took a deep breath and thrust himself up out of the water as far as he could. He willed himself up and over and almost made an arc, but then did a belly flop into the water. The dolphins helped him surface, gently pushing him up with their sleek bodies, and politely didn't laugh at him. They encouraged him to have another go, and then another, trying to surface and turn their somersaults in slow motion to show Milo how to do it.

He did his best to copy them, trying hard, and eventually got the knack. Milo went up in the air, held his body taut, and then dived elegantly back into the water with scarcely a ripple. The dolphins *eeked* loudly in praise and slapped their flippers against their sides in applause.

There was more applause from the shallows from Birdy and the Faraway Tree folk. All the little squirrels tried to copy him, tumbling up and down and making a terrific splash. Milo clapped them in turn and then joined the dolphins again to swim in a circle with them. They all surfaced together, drops of water sparkling on three grey bodies and one pink one as they rose in the air and then dived down again.

The next time Milo surfaced he trod water and checked on Mia. She was near enough to see him and risked letting go of the sea unicorn's mane for a moment to give him a hearty clap.

Milo felt like a king of the sea with Mia the queen. Birdy was perfectly happy being the princess of paddling. Silky tried to show her how to swim, gently holding Birdy round her waist and supporting her chin so she wouldn't get her face wet, but she couldn't manage more than two strokes of doggy-paddle.

'I'm not one for swimming either, Birdy,' said Moonface. 'Try floating – it's far less strenuous. Look, like this.' He waded out a little further, then threw himself on his back with his arms and legs spread wide, his round tummy in the air. Birdy wasn't at all sure about this, but bravely decided to have a go. She lay on her back, stuck her tummy out and made little paddles of her hands. It was surprisingly easy. She laughed in delight.

'Look at me!' she called.

'Well done, Birdy!' Moonface and Silky chorused.

Birdy put her foot down to the sand underneath to make sure she wasn't drifting out of her depth, and then floated happily up and down on the waves. She looked up at the dazzling sky, her heart thumping with pride. She hoped Milo and Mia might be watching.

'I'm floating and it's easy-peasy!' she called, in case they were nearby.

'Yes, it is – but it's clever of you to manage without a tail,' someone said.

Birdy tried to turn her head sideways to see who it was, and immediately sank herself. She went under the water, spluttering, but firm small hands gripped her and helped her up again.

'Thank you, Silky,' she said, blinking and coughing.

'I'm not Silky,' said the someone.

Birdy rubbed her eyes. She was looking at a small girl about her own age, with long, wavy hair right down to her waist. The water was so clear, Birdy could see *below* her waist too. This girl didn't have legs. She had a shimmering green tail divided into two at the end.

'Oh, you lucky thing! You've got a mermaid tail! Did you get it at that lovely, big shop?' she asked.

'You don't buy tails at a shop!' said the girl, laughing so that she showed her perfect, pearly teeth. 'You just get born with one! Mine's not fully grown yet, so I can't swim as far as my sisters, but I can make fantastic ripples. Watch!'

The mermaid lay on her back, her hair drifting out in a halo round her head. She raised her beautiful tail and flipped it firmly on the surface of the water. Ripples spread all the way to the shore, splashing the squirrels again.

'See!' said the mermaid proudly. 'I bet you wish you could do it!'

'Yes, I do – but I can kick!' said Birdy. She lay back too and kicked her legs up and down as hard as she could. She couldn't really make ripples, but she was an excellent splasher and they both got very wet in the face.

'You have excellent legs!' said the mermaid. 'Can you walk very far on them?'

'Yes, I could walk all the way along this great, big beach and back again, and I can run quite fast and skip and dance a bit too,' said Birdy.

'I can't walk or run or skip – but I *can* dance,' said the mermaid. 'Watch.'

She composed herself and then drifted through the water very gracefully to the left and the right, and then she twirled round and round, pointing her tail.

'Oh, that's lovely. I can't dance like that. I do

the jumping-up-and-down sort,' said Birdy, demonstrating.

'That looks so funny!' said the mermaid. 'Can you sing too?'

'Yep,' said Birdy, which wasn't strictly true. She had difficulty remembering all the words to songs, and sometimes made up her own tunes by mistake. Still, there was one song she knew by heart.

'We wish you a merry Christmas,
We wish you a merry Christmas,
We wish you a merry Christmas,
And a happy New Year!'

The mermaid seemed delighted. 'What an original song! It's so jolly. All our mermaid songs are sad.' She tossed her long hair behind her shoulders, and started singing, looking very solemn.

Birdy wasn't musical, but she knew the mermaid's song was the most beautiful music she'd ever heard, so strange and haunting that she shivered in spite of the bright sunshine.

'That's so lovely!' Birdy said. 'I can't believe I'm actually playing with a real mermaid! What's your name? I'm Birdy. It's a funny name, isn't it? I bet you've never met a Birdy before.'

'I'm Coral,' she said. 'It's not a very distinctive name at all. A lot of mermaids are called Coral, because our palaces are built on coral reefs.'

'You live in a palace! Are you a princess mermaid?' Birdy asked in awe.

'No!' said Coral, giggling. 'I haven't got a crown, have I? My father works as a breakfast chef in the palace. He's famous for his seaweed croissants and his limpet muesli. You should try them!'

'Mmm,' said Birdy, who privately thought they sounded disgusting. She had always wanted to be a mermaid, but perhaps it wasn't such a good idea if that was the sort of thing they ate. 'Does your mother cook too?'

'She's a hairdresser,' said Coral. 'She doesn't get to style the royal family's hair, but she's very busy with all the other mermaids. She does my hair too, but she gets cross with me because it's always in a tangle.'

'Oh, my mum moans about *my* tangles!' said Birdy. 'She's a teacher, but not at my school, thank goodness!'

'Is your father a teacher too?' Coral asked.

'He teaches woodwork,' said Birdy. 'He loves making things. He made me my own doll's house. And he said he'd make me and my brother and sister a sledge for this winter, but he hasn't got round to it so far, and anyway, we haven't had any snow yet, worse luck. It's just ever so windy and rainy and cold.'

'Windy and rainy and cold,' said Coral wonderingly. 'With no sunshine at all? But the sea's still warm, isn't it?'

'No, it's absolutely freezing!' said Birdy.

'I always wished I could be a human child, but I can't imagine swimming in a *cold* sea!' said Coral. 'Don't you find it very unpleasant?'

'I don't do it!' said Birdy. 'In fact I can't swim at all. But I can float! Watch!'

She demonstrated, hoping she hadn't lost the

knack. Luckily she lay as comfortably on top of the water as if she were lying on her own bed.

'Excellent,' said Coral kindly, who had been floating since she was a few days old. 'Let me teach you how to swim. It's so easy when you know how, I promise.'

Birdy was extremely doubtful. Silky had had no luck at all teaching her. But Coral simply ducked her head and dived downwards, her long hair streaming behind her, and Birdy felt compelled to follow her. She held out her arms like Coral and found she could swoop herself forward. She didn't have a long tail to flip, but she could kick her legs – and there she was, swimming!

The beach seemed to suddenly slope dramatically, because Birdy found herself swimming down and down and down, somehow holding her breath. Coral took hold of her hand and pointed even further down. Birdy found she could see through the crystal clear water, and far away she made out the spires and turrets of a great underwater palace – Coral's home!

She badly wanted to swim all the way down to it, but Coral shook her head, her hair swirling like golden seaweed, and then gently urged her upwards again. Birdy swam up, thrilled that she could hold her breath for so long, but when her head burst out of the water into the sunshine she found she was gasping for air.

'I wanted to see inside your palace!' she spluttered.

'You can't live underwater, Birdy – and I can't live on land,' said Coral regretfully. 'I wish we could play together for longer, but I can only stay up in the air a little while.' She looked back at the beach. There seemed to be a lot of activity, with folk digging in the sand.

Birdy looked too. 'What are they doing?'

'I think they're making sandcastles,' said Coral. 'It looks such fun. Why don't you go and join in, Birdy?'

'No, I want to stay with you!' said Birdy. 'I can dig a sandcastle any old time. We've even got a sandpit at school.'

'I think you'll find this sand is different,' said

Coral. 'And I'm afraid I have to go. My mother will be getting worried as I've been gone so long.'

'My mum doesn't even know I'm here, but she won't worry because time stands still in the Enchanted Wood,' said Birdy.

'I wish time stood still here,' said Coral. 'Especially today. The Land of Sunshine moves on soon, and it makes the sea so choppy that we can barely swim.'

Birdy wasn't listening properly. She was just so pleased that she had learnt to swim herself.

'I can't wait to show Milo and Mia,' Birdy said. 'I must be a much better swimmer than they are if I can dive so far down! Will you come back and play with me this afternoon, Coral?'

'I'm not sure I can,' said Coral regretfully.

'But will I see you again?' Birdy asked.

'I hope so,' said Coral. 'Anyway, let's exchange hair bracelets!' She plucked a few strands of her shining hair, twisted them in some magic intricate way and wound them round Birdy's wrist, tying the ends neatly.

'Awesome!' said Birdy. She tried hard to pull several hairs from her own head, but it hurt!

'This way,' said Coral, and she managed to ease out a few hairs from Birdy's head with her hardly noticing.

Birdy tried to plait the hairs, but she hadn't quite mastered the art and they kept twiddling around.

'Shall I help?' Coral asked tactfully. She took Birdy's flimsy lock and neatly plaited it in a second, fastened it round her wrist and held it out for Birdy to tie the final knot in the bow.

Birdy hadn't learnt to tie a neat bow yet either. 'Left over right – or is it right over left?' she muttered. At least she knew her left from her right, because she always sucked her left thumb rather than her right. She didn't know why, it just felt more comforting.

'There!' Birdy said triumphantly, when she'd managed it. 'Does this mean we're best friends now?'

'Yes, best friends for ever!' said Coral.

Birdy's heart nearly burst with joy. She was best friends with a fairy *and* a mermaid!

CHAPTER FIVE

BIRDY AND Coral gave each other a hug, and then the little mermaid swam further out to sea, turned to give one last wave and dived downwards. Birdy sighed and started wading back to the sand.

Milo was just coming out of the sea too, a little further down. They ran to each other.

'You'll never guess who I've been swimming with!' they burst out simultaneously.

They kicked their way to the shore, making great plumes of spray, as they talked mermaids and dolphins.

'Poor Mia! She just got to ride on that sea

unicorn, and she's done that already,' said Birdy.

But when Mia came splashing up, joining them, she looked incredibly happy.

'I'm so sorry I was gone so long! You must have been really worried. But it was just so wonderful,' Mia said dreamily. 'Did you see? My unicorn came specially to find me! Did you see us surfing the waves?'

'Did you see me actually swimming with *dolphins*?' said Milo.

'Did you see me actually swimming with a *mermaid*?' said Birdy.

They chattered non-stop on the sand, drying off in moments as they walked up and down looking at everyone's sandcastles. Silky was making a very tall tower with dark green seaweed winding round its walls like ivy. There was a window right at the top that had a little sand model inside, with long, curly yellow seaweed trailing down to the ground.

'Rapunzel!' said Birdy. 'Oh, Silky, she's awesome!'

'I wish you'd find another word instead of awesome, Birdy!' said Milo – but he had to admit

Silky's elaborate tower really *was* awesome.

Moonface was busy making a huge castle. He had commanded a troop of tiny squirrels to help him with the hard labour, pinching the ridges on the top of the walls with their dextrous little paws. Moonface himself was jabbing the slits for windows, chuckling each time he did it. Sometimes he jabbed so hard the sand started crumbling and he had to build the wall up again, but he pretended he was simply testing it for strength.

'What do you think, Birdy?' Moonface said. 'Isn't my castle awesome?'

'You bet!' said Birdy. '*Utterly* awesome!'

Dame Washalot and Dame Ironallday had made two cosy cottages next to each other, decorated with shells. They each had a very neat seaweed garden with tiny pebble paths to the front door.

'Oh, dames, they look lovely,' said Mia tactfully, though she actually preferred Silky's tower and Moonface's castle.

'We're planning to retire soon and live in two little cottages like these!' said Dame Washalot. She looked at her poor hands, red and sore from scrubbing clothes clean endlessly in her washtub. 'No more washing! We'll send our clothes to the laundry!'

'We won't even own an iron!' said Dame Ironallday. 'Who cares about creases and crumples! Can't wait!'

The Saucepan Man and Mr Watzisname were also working on a joint project – a huge boat that they could both fit inside.

'Two friends with a sand boat,
Two seats side by side,
We'll make sure we float
And row far and wide!'

The Saucepan Man sang his song happily and Mr Watzisname whistled an accompaniment as they smoothed the sides of the boat with their spades.

'You can come and join us for company,' Mr Watzisname told the Angry Pixie.

'Thanks, but no thanks,' said the Angry Pixie, who was digging furiously, spraying everyone with sand as he made a huge hole.

'Are you making an underground tunnel, Mr Pixie?' Milo asked. He never knew quite how to address him. He might think *Pixie* was a little too curt, like calling a teacher by their surname – yet *Angry* sounded rather rude. The Angry Pixie was usually very quick to take offence and would get in a rage and pour a jug of water over you. Milo spotted he had a handy bucket of water by his side and stepped back quickly.

However, the Land of Sunshine seemed to be working its magic. The Angry Pixie smiled pleasantly.

'I'm making an underground *dwelling*, Mr Milo, so far down that no one will ever disturb me. I shall snooze in the dark all day in perfect peace,' he said.

'I like to snooze in the dark too, in my bear cave!' said Pippin. 'But then I like to come out and visit my special friends!'

'We love to visit you too, dearest Pippin,' said Mia, giving him a big hug, though he was still very sticky from his sun lotion.

Milo and Birdy joined in the hug too.

'How are you doing, little Pip?' said Milo.

'We've missed you so much!' said Birdy.

'You're not the only one! I've missed you too!' said Pippin. He counted on his little claws. 'No, I've missed you *three*! I shall give a party for you. Yes, four, counting me!' He laughed so much that he rolled on the sand, all four paws in the air, and knocked his sunhat off.

'Hey, you'd better put your hat on again, or Silky will get cross with you!' said Mia. 'So what are you making?'

Pippin hadn't needed to dig with a spade. His claws were very efficient. He'd built a big, round sandcastle, but it didn't seem to have any doors or windows. The children all stared at it, mystified.

'Can't you guess?' said Pippin. 'It's a giant pot of honey! So what are you going to make?'

The children thought hard. They'd made sandcastles before, even Birdy, but they weren't very good at it. Dad had generally given them a hand with the digging and Mum had helped with the decorating. All the Faraway Tree folk were so good at sand modelling! The children felt their own contributions would look utterly pathetic by comparison.

Even the squirrels had made a magnificent sand tree that stood way above their heads, with little holes here and there so they could all squeeze in the tree together.

'How do they make it stand *up* like that?' said Milo.

'With all those little squirrels jumping about in it too?' said Mia.

'My sandcastles always fall down,' said Birdy. 'Even the ones I make with a bucket.'

But when they settled down to try to make their own sandcastles they understood. The sand near the water's edge was the perfect consistency for building. It was light and easy to dig, and yet it moulded together like dough. They found they could fashion it any way they wanted. Sometimes they had only to lay their hands in the sand and think hard and the sand sprang into shape with barely a twitch of their fingers.

Milo made a dolphin out of sand, with little white seashell teeth. It was big and strong enough for Milo to climb on its back. Mia was encouraged to try to make a unicorn, though that would be bigger still, and have four legs and a long horn. It seemed impossible, but she found the sand wonderfully pliable. A model of a sea unicorn emerged from the sand, not life-size, which might have been too ambitious, but a very accurate miniature, with a long seaweed mane and tail. Its skin even had a pearly sheen like the real sea unicorn. Mia stroked it lovingly, murmuring to it.

Birdy made a mermaid just like Coral, using yet more seaweed for her long hair. Her tail was a challenge, but she collected little, shiny, flat pebbles from the water's edge and studded them all along her tail so that they shone like scales. She made her mermaid lying down on the sand because the tip of her tail wasn't strong enough to support her. Then Birdy lay down beside the mermaid, keeping her company. She put her heels together and stuck her feet out, so that they resembled a tail too.

'We're two mermaids floating in the sea,' Birdy announced happily.

There was a ringing of a handbell and a line of helpful elves in uniform came marching over the sands, carrying wicker baskets and trays of iced drinks in different colours.

'Picnic time, everyone!' the elves chorused.

They'd bought magnificent treats for everyone according to taste. Silky had glistening green asparagus spears with hollandaise sauce and an exquisite plate of red and black berries arranged in an elaborate pattern, with an outer ring of deep pink watermelon, and a glass of raspberry cordial. Moonface had platters of cheese and meat and fish, with chunks of crusty bread and a pot of butter, and an enormous apple pie all to himself, with ice cream piled on top. It stayed firm and icy cold, even in the strong sunshine. He had lemonade to wash it all down.

The Saucepan Man and Mr Watzisname and the

THE MAGIC FARAWAY TREE

Angry Pixie had veal and ham pie and boiled eggs and sausages and spicy salads and suet tart with custard cream, and apple-cider to drink. The dames had cold chicken with tomatoes and potato salad and strawberry meringue and iced lemon tea. Pippin had honey sandwiches cut into tiny triangles, and honey cakes with little sugary teddy bears on top, and honeydew melon, and rosehip syrupy juice in a feeder cup so that he didn't spill it all down his front. The squirrels had nut roast with a green salad, and hazelnut ice cream, and almond milk.

The children shrieked with delight when they saw what was in *their* hamper. They had slices of cheese pizza with smiley faces made from black olive eyes, pepperoni noses and red tomato mouths, tiny hot dogs with tomato sauce, giant crisps in different flavours, shiny red apples and banoffee pie.

'All our favourite foods!' said Mia.

'And we know what you'd like to drink too!' the elves chorused. 'Ginger beer!'

The children stared at them blankly. Then they stared at the tray of glasses filled with strange brownish liquid.

'We're not allowed to drink beer!' said Birdy.

'I don't think it's real beer,' said Mia.

'I think I've had it once,' said Milo. He lowered his voice. 'I didn't like the taste much.'

They stared at the ginger beer without enthusiasm, though they tried hard to keep polite smiles on their faces.

'The other children who come here love their ginger beer. They drink *lashings* of it! But perhaps you'd prefer cola instead?' the chief elf suggested.

The children nodded hopefully, and another elf came trotting up, with glasses of dark, sparkling drink, clinking with ice cubes in the shape of tiny cola cans.

'Ah!' said the elves happily, as the children thanked them and drank eagerly. And ate and ate and ate. The squirrels ate, Pippin ate, the dames ate, the gentlemen ate, Moonface ate and Silky ate (albeit daintily).

'Now can we go swimming again?' Mia asked, hoping her sea unicorn might come back for her.

'I should wait and let your meal go down first,' said Silky. 'Though if you're going to sunbathe, rub on some factor fifty so you don't burn.' (Occasionally Silky sounded rather like Mum.)

'Oh, I want to swim with my dolphin mates,' said Milo.

'And I want to meet up with my best friend, Coral,' said Birdy.

But they were all feeling rather full so they didn't argue too much. They found three sun-loungers close together, obediently lathered themselves with sunblock and lay down.

'We won't actually go to sleep though, will we?' said Birdy. 'We could sing Christmassy songs. Except it doesn't really feel like Christmas here, does it?'

'It feels a lot better than it does in the Enchanted Wood!' said Milo.

'I wish we could stay in the Land of Sunshine for ever, and then I could ride my unicorn every single day,' said Mia, yawning suddenly.

They were all yawning now – and in two minutes they were all fast asleep. Everyone on the beach enjoyed a little post-picnic nap, even the squirrels, who all curled up in the shade inside their sand tree. Pippin lay underneath his sun-lounger so that he was totally in the shade. The dames pulled their mob caps right down over their noses. The Saucepan Man used one of his own kitchen utensils as a sunhat. Mr Watzisname started snoring very loudly, his mouth wide open. The Angry Pixie sighed happily in his sleep, so contented that he wondered if he'd have to change his name to the Tranquil Pixie. Moonface felt his white face glowing and wondered if he'd have to change his name too. He dozed off, muttering, 'Sunface,' to himself. Silky lay on her tummy with her gossamer wings spread out. She waved them gently to make a little breeze, sighing contentedly in her sleep.

It was Mia who woke up first. She rubbed her eyes and stared out to sea, looking for her unicorn. The sea was no longer smooth and still. There were big waves, all of them crested with foam.

'Hey, Milo, wake up!' she said. 'I think my unicorn's coming for me again, making another huge great wave!'

Milo opened his eyes and peered out to sea. 'There are far too many waves. I think it's all the dolphins!'

'Maybe it's lots and lots of mermaids,' Birdy murmured hopefully, still half asleep.

'The sea's really choppy now!' said Mia.

Birdy vaguely remembered Coral telling her that the sea could get too choppy for swimming. Now why was that? Suddenly she remembered!

'The Land of Sunshine's moving on!' Birdy shouted, so loudly that everyone on the beach woke up with a start.

Milo and Mia and Birdy spent two seconds wondering if they really wanted to stay in the Land of Sunshine for ever. It was such a beautiful land where nothing bad could ever happen. They could ride on sea horses, swim with dolphins and make friends with mermaids. They could eat their favourite food, and have two or more ice creams a day. They had each other, so they could never feel lonely. But in spite of all this, it wasn't *home*, with Mum and Dad.

Suddenly they knew for certain that they absolutely had to get back down the Faraway Tree!

Everyone else felt the same and sprang into action. They jumped off their sun-loungers and started running this way and that, forgetting where the vital ladder was that would lead them back through the clouds to the Enchanted Forest.

'No! No! *This* way!' Silky shouted. 'It's right over there, behind the big white building! Follow me!' She flew up in the air so that she could guide them all properly. Milo and Mia held hands with Birdy and Pippin and ran with them, tugging them so quickly that their feet and paws barely touched the sand. The dames ran together, holding their skirts up so they wouldn't stumble. The Saucepan Man and Mr Watzisname and the Angry Pixie charged along in a line, puffing hard. Moonface bravely scurried to the sand treehouse and made sure every little squirrel had jumped out before he set off too.

The sand started to shift alarmingly, little hillocks and valleys appearing in the smooth surface. It made running fast much harder, and several stumbled. The littlest squirrels panicked and started darting this way and that, running the wrong way in their confusion. Mr Red went after the littlest, but two more were veering off in different directions.

Moonface began running after them, but his little legs were stiff and slow.

'I can catch one. I can run the fastest!' said Milo.

'I'll get the other. I can run just as fast!' said Mia. 'Birdy, Pippin, run towards Silky – and get down that ladder!'

'But we want to wait for you!' said Birdy. 'What if you don't make it in time?'

'We will, I promise!' said Milo. 'Now *run*!' He pushed them both hard and then started haring after the tiniest squirrel. It fell down the Angry Pixie's big hole in the sand and vanished.

Milo blinked, wondering what had happened. The tiny squirrel seemed to have disappeared. 'Squirrel! Little squirrel! Where *are* you?' Milo called desperately, running backwards and forwards.

The tiny squirrel managed a faint cheep. Milo stopped in his tracks.

'Squirrel? Please call louder so I can find you!' he cried.

The squirrel had had all the wind knocked out of him when he fell into the hole. He sat up, filled his small lungs and squealed with all his might. Milo ran towards the sound, saw the hole and threw himself down on to the shifting sand. He reached right into the hole and managed to grasp the tiny creature's waving paw. He hauled it out, tucked it down his shirt and ran for the ladder.

Mia meanwhile had snatched the other squirrel up in her arms – but in her terror the squirrel scrambled away, squeaking piteously, looking for her mother. Mia darted after her and managed to grab her all over again. 'Don't worry, we'll find your mother, but we must go now. Hang on tight!' she managed to reassure her as she hurtled towards the ladder.

Milo got to the ladder first, thrust his baby squirrel into Dame Washalot's arms and went back to help Mia. The land was tipping in a terrifying manner now, creating a sand storm, and the waves were crashing violently on the shore.

The sand got in Mia's eyes so that she couldn't see where she was going, but Milo reached her and pulled her along. The sand was blowing so hard now that they could barely stagger, but Silky swooped down and somehow managed to lift them all, two children and one squirming squirrel, and fly them to the ladder just as it was disappearing. They tumbled downwards, feeling for the rungs, and Silky landed lightly on top of them as the Land of Sunshine broke away completely.

CHAPTER
SIX

THEY HURLED themselves down the ladder, and everyone landed safely in the strong wide branches of the Magic Faraway Tree. They gasped in the sudden cold and wet of the bleak December day.

'Everyone, back to my place because it's the biggest!' Moonface called. 'I'll light a huge fire and we'll all huddle round it and drink hot chocolate and get warm.'

It seemed a marvellous idea. Everyone hurried to Moonface's round house, Milo and Mia and Birdy, Silky, Pippin, the two dames, the three gentlemen and a very large scurry of squirrels. Their teeth were chattering, so they sounded rather like a percussion band.

It wasn't until everyone was sitting on every sofa, chair, cushion and rug sipping hot chocolate that Silky gently slid three tiny squirrels from her lap and looked down at herself and then at everyone else.

'We're still in our Land of Sunshine beach outfits!' she cried.

There was general consternation. Birdy couldn't understand what all the fuss was about.

'I like my summer dress much better than my boring old jeans and jumper!' she said. 'And I never liked my coat anyway because the zip is a bit scratchy under my chin.'

'But we can't go home like this, Birdy!' said Mia. 'What on earth will Mum and Dad say? They'll wonder what on earth we've done with our winter clothes. If we tell them the absolute truth, they'll never believe us – and if they do, they'll worry so and never let us go in the Enchanted Wood again.'

'And it's going to be absolutely freezing going

home in these clothes!' said Milo.

Silky was able to shut her eyes, concentrate hard and somehow magic her dress and wings back to her silver winter-wear.

'Show us how to do that, Silky!' said Milo.

'I wish I could, but I can only work magic on myself. My powers increase on Christmas Eve – but we can't wait that long. You're all shivering! Moonface, you're the one who spent years at Enchanter School. Could you possibly magic everyone's winter clothes back?' Silky asked, rather doubtfully.

'Of course I can – easy-peasy!' said Moonface. 'I know the changing clothes rhyme off by heart! It's one of the first spells we learnt.

'Change back all clothes
From top to toes.
For all of those,
When I wiggle my . . .

'Now what was it I had to wiggle? My ears?'

Moonface tried flapping his pointy ears, but nothing happened.

'When I wiggle my bottom!' said Pippin, and he and the squirrels squealed with laughter.

'When I wiggle my *nose!*' the three children shouted together.

'That's it! The very one,' said Moonface. He wiggled his nose energetically, his white face flushing pink with effort.

Everyone's beach clothes vanished – to be replaced by winter clothing. But perhaps Moonface had wiggled his nose *too* vigorously. Silky stayed in her own beautiful silver outfit, but everyone else ended up in the *wrong* winter clothes! Milo found he was wearing Mia's clothes and Mia found she was wearing Milo's. This didn't really matter, because Mia was almost as tall as Milo now, and they liked wearing the same sort of clothes anyway. But Birdy found she was wearing Pippin's very sticky jumper, which was much too big for her because he was such a stout little bear. His head was much bigger than hers too, so his woolly bobble hat came right down to her nose. Her own hat was perched on one of Pippin's ears, and her jumpers were stretched to bursting point over his furry chest. They fell about laughing at each other, and then laughed even more when they looked at the others.

Dame Washalot was dressed as the Saucepan Man, clanking with all his bulky kitchenware – and Dame Ironallday was in Mr Watzisname's natty corduroy suit and cream raincoat. The two gentlemen were wearing the dames' frilly mob caps and their knitted cardies and flouncy skirts and petticoats. Moonface had even managed to muddle his own

clothes with those of the Angry Pixie's and wore his little red outfit, which was much too small, and his long, pointy boots, which were much too big. The Angry Pixie wore Moonface's jacket and checked trousers, with Moonface's little polished shoes stuck on the end of his long, pointy feet. The squirrels all wore hats and mufflers in the winter, but they liked different colours, so there was a great deal of swapping going on.

Silky sorted out Birdy and Pippin, and Moonface changed clothes with the Angry Pixie in a matter of moments, both chuckling merrily. Maybe the Angry Pixie had become permanently happy now? The Saucepan Man and Mr Watzisname were much less happy in their dame clothes and Dame Washalot couldn't wait to rid herself of all those clanking saucepans and kettles – but Dame Ironallday rather fancied herself in Mr Watzisname's suit and smart raincoat and he had to persuade her to return them.

They were all worn out by the time everyone was back in their own clothes, but Moonface handed out his special Toffee Shocks as refreshments. The children had forgotten how delicious they were, the toffee getting more and more wondrously tasty, and growing in their mouths every time they chewed, so they could only go *ooble ooble ooble* if they tried to talk to each other. Then the gigantic toffee suddenly popped inside their mouths, giving them a shock in delight.

'Do you think we could have another one? And another after that, like in the Land of Sunshine?' Birdy whispered.

'Probably not,' Milo whispered back, regretfully. He looked at his watch out of habit – and saw that it was only ten past nine in the morning.

'It looks as if time still stops here in the Enchanted Wood,' he said.

'Even so, we'd better get back to the cottage,' said Mia. 'Suppose your watch has just gone wrong, and Mum and Dad are going frantic, wondering where we've been all day.'

'I want Mum and Dad,' Birdy said. 'I thought I was going to get stuck in the Land of Sunshine and I'd never see them again.' She paused. Her chin started wobbling and her eyes went watery. 'It was my fault. Coral warned me that the Land of Sunshine was going to move, but I was having such a lovely time I forgot to tell anyone.' Tears started splashing down her cheeks.

'Don't worry, Birdy. It wasn't your fault, honestly,' said Milo, putting his arm round her.

'And you were the one who woke everyone up. We'd have all been whirled away if it wasn't for you. Don't cry, little Bird,' said Mia, dabbing at Birdy's cheeks.

They sometimes forgot Birdy was smaller than them and took things to heart.

'We'll go back to the cottage right away,' said Milo. 'This very minute.'

'Perhaps in *five* minutes,' said Birdy. She wanted Mum and Dad badly, but she also wanted to wait just in case Moonface offered his tin of Toffee Shocks round the room again.

'Would you three like another Toffee Shock to chew on your way home?' Moonface said immediately, as if he could read Birdy's mind. He sometimes muddled his magic spells, but he was very clever at knowing how to please children. 'Try my new variety – they're especially long lasting,' he said, reaching for another tin on his shelves.

The new Toffee Shocks came in various flavours. Birdy chose a yellow banana-flavoured Toffee Shock. Mia chose a red raspberry-flavoured Toffee Shock. Milo chose a brown chocolate-flavoured Toffee Shock. They were all absolutely delicious and started getting bigger at the very first chew. They found they could barely speak as they said their goodbyes to everyone.

'An we ome and ee ou oomorrow?' Birdy asked Silky as she hugged her.

'Of course you can!' said Silky, laughing. 'Shall I come with you now and show you the way through the wood?'

'Oh, let me take them!' Pippin begged. 'I know the way back to front! I never get lost now, do I?'

'You're a very clever little bear. And perhaps Moonface will let you have one of his new Toffee Shocks to see you on your way?' said Silky.

Pippin was very happy to be offered one. He chose a beige honey-flavoured Toffee Shock and crammed it into his mouth greedily. Then he went to the hole in the middle of Moonface's floor, sat on a cushion and started whizzing down the slippery-slip slide. Mia went next and Milo went last, with Birdy on his lap because she was always just a little bit scared of going down the slippery-slip by herself.

Mr Red came down too, and collected up all the cushions as they came flying out of the trapdoor at the bottom of the tree, so they wouldn't get wet. It was still pouring with rain. The children stared at the relentless raindrops, trying to will them to turn into snow. It was certainly cold enough for snow, and it struck them as colder still after the wonderful warmth of the Land of Sunshine.

Pippin didn't seem to mind. He ran right round the Faraway Tree and back again, jumping in the puddles joyfully.

'Oh, lovely rain again!' he said.

His thick, dark fur was waterproof, so the rain

streamed off him, though a little drip clung to his funny little snout. The children were very much *not* waterproof, and were soaked right through in a few seconds.

'Can you stop playing, Pippin, and point us in the right direction?' Milo asked.

'He's just having fun,' said Mia. 'It was far too hot for him in the Land of Sunshine.'

'It wasn't too hot for me,' said Birdy. 'And I could always cool down having a swim with my best friend Coral.' She stroked the hair friendship bracelet wound about her wrist and sighed. 'I shall *miss* Coral,' she said.

'I know. I'll miss my unicorn terribly,' said Mia, and she sighed too.

'Maybe the Land of Unicorns will come back and you'll see him then,' said Milo. 'Come on, Pippin, please! We're getting soaking here!'

'It's such fun,' said Pippin, jumping in the biggest puddle and splashing them all. He chuckled wickedly, but then calmed down and scampered off. 'This way!' he called.

They wondered if he was still teasing them because they didn't recognise the path at all. And the first time they'd encountered Pippin in the Enchanted Wood he'd been as lost as they were, so perhaps he wasn't the most reliable guide. But they followed him nevertheless – and in a matter of moments the trees started thinning out, and they found themselves back by the ditch.

They thanked the little bear, feeling ashamed for doubting him.

'You'll be able to find your own way back, won't you?' said Mia.

'It's easy-peasy!' Pippin said. 'See you tomorrow?'

'Definitely!' said Milo.

They waved goodbye and Pippin waved both his paws back at them and then scampered off. They jumped over the ditch and ran back to the cottage. Their tummies started churning. They couldn't tell if they'd been gone only a few minutes in real time – or a whole day. It was so dark and dreary that it seemed like dusk already.

But when they went rushing in the back door

Mum and Dad were there in the cold kitchen, still drinking their second cups of coffee.

'Oh, goodness, look at the state of you!' said Mum, rushing for towels.

'Why didn't you come back straight away, you silly kids!' said Dad. 'You look like drowned rats! What were you *doing* out there?'

'Just having fun,' said Milo, his teeth chattering. 'I'd forgotten how freezing cold it is in the cottage.'

'Let's get you out of those sodden clothes then,' said Mum. 'I've found an emergency plumber and he's promised to come out this morning. I do hope he can mend the wretched boiler. If not, we'll simply have to go home again.'

'Oh, no! We can't go home! We don't mind the cold, do we?' said Mia, though she was shivering violently.

'We love it,' said Birdy, though she was grey-blue with cold and her teeth were chattering.

They were all desperate. They couldn't possibly go home when they'd only just got here. They'd had the most fantastic time up the Faraway Tree already and they were determined to have day after day of fun there with all their friends.

'You're a funny lot,' said Dad fondly, towelling Mia's sopping hair.

'A very silly lot!' said Mum, wrapping Birdy up like a baby in the biggest towel. 'Still, you're warming up already, darling. You've got lovely, rosy cheeks. And a rosy nose too!'

'Like Rudolph,' said Milo, who liked to towel himself.

Birdy opened her mouth to start singing 'Rudolph the Red-Nosed Reindeer', but they all begged her not to. Once would be fine, but Birdy only seemed to sing on repeat mode.

Mum was staring at her, looking puzzled. Then she looked at Milo and Mia.

'You've *all* got red faces!' she said. 'It looks as if you've been sunbathing!'

'They're just chapped from the wind,' Mia said quickly.

'Well, we'd better stay indoors today,' said Dad. 'Though I wish it were warmer. Perhaps I'd better go foraging for broken branches in the Enchanted Wood to keep the fire burning all day long.'

The children looked alarmed and hoped Dad would forget this idea. Wonderfully, the plumber came knocking at the door of the cottage just then. Mum and Dad greeted him enthusiastically, plying him with cups of tea and a couple of the mince pies Mum had brought from home. He set to work on the boiler, surprised at its age, and not sure he'd have the right parts with him in his van – but by half past ten he'd got the boiler working again. Mum actually gave him a hug and Dad gave him a very big Christmas tip and within half an hour the cottage started to feel cosy again, though it was still pouring with rain outside.

The children flopped around happily enough, tired after their exciting day in the sunshine and the sea. Mum read her book and Dad started whittling at a thick stick, turning it deftly this way and that till it started to take shape.

'Is it an animal?' said Birdy.

'Yep,' said Dad.

'It looks like . . . a little bear!' she said.

'Brilliant girl,' said Dad.

'It's Pippin, isn't it?' said Birdy.

Mia and Milo froze.

'Who's Pippin?' Dad asked.

'You know!' said Birdy, though of course Dad didn't know Pippin.

Birdy looked at Mia and Milo. They shook their heads, pulling faces at her. Birdy remembered she had to keep Pippin a secret.

'Ah! Er . . . Pippin's my pretend friend. He's a little bear just like that,' she said.

'You and your imagination, Birdy,' said Dad.

Birdy grinned, proud of herself for saving the day. Even she could tell that Dad and Mum would never in a million years let her play with a brown bear cub with a full set of teeth and claws.

They had cheesy baked potatoes for lunch, with a mince pie and clementines for pudding. The children were surprisingly hungry, even though they had eaten several ice creams and a big picnic lunch already.

'The rain's actually stopping now,' said Dad, peering out of the window. 'Let's go for that walk in the wood to walk off our lunch.'

The children looked at each other in alarm. It was their wood, their Magic Faraway Tree, their friends. They weren't at all sure Dad and Mum would get on with them all – and they certainly wouldn't let them climb a tree that reached right up to the clouds.

Mum didn't seem too keen on the idea either.

'You go with the kids. I'd sooner lie here on the sofa and finish my book,' she said.

'OK. Come on then, you lot. Collect your coats and woollies from the radiators. They're all warm and dry now. Let's look for wood!'

'You can't burn wood when it's wet, Dad,' said Milo.

'And the trees will still drip on us even if it's stopped raining,' said Mia.

'And there might be big, bad wolves in the wood,' said Birdy, pretending to be frightened.

Dad just laughed at them, refusing to be deterred,

so they very reluctantly put their winter clothes on all over again. They went out of the back door, walked a few paces down the lane and then Dad jumped over the ditch into the Enchanted Wood. The children held their breath.

'Jump over then,' said Dad, puzzled. He reached out his hands to Birdy. 'Come on, little chickie, I'll help you.'

'I can do it myself, Dad,' said Birdy.

'Birdy!' Milo warned.

'I mean, I'm sure I can do it,' Birdy added quickly. 'Look! Wheee!' She jumped over, and Milo and Mia jumped too.

'What are we going to do if Pippin comes running up?' Mia whispered.

'Or Silky flies overhead or a squirrel comes whizzing out of the slippery-slip!' Milo muttered.

But none of these things happened. The wood seemed to have lost all its enchantment. The trees rustled a little, but still didn't make their *wisha-wisha-wisha* sound. Several rabbits ran away from them, their white fluffy tails bobbing in the dim light, and a fawn hovered nearby, ears alert, but they didn't try to speak. Squirrels ran up and down the trees, chattering loudly, but in their own animal language.

They trudged through the muddy grass for a very long time, until the trees started thinning out at the other side, but they somehow missed the Magic Faraway Tree altogether. It was a relief, but the children couldn't help worrying. It was still *there*, wasn't it? It hadn't been suddenly whisked away like the magic lands above it?

'What's up with you lot?' Dad asked, as he busily gathered large sticks for kindling, and smaller bendy sticks for Mum to make into a Christmas wreath. 'You've gone very quiet.'

'We're just a bit tired, Dad, that's all,' said Milo.

Dad tutted. 'I thought you were all super-fit, racing around in the morning!'

This was annoying, because they'd climbed an amazingly tall tree and then swum energetically for ages, but they couldn't explain. Dad saw they were all drooping now and took pity on them.

'Milo, Mia, you two carry all the wood, while I give Birdy a piggyback. We'll go to the cottage now, and all have a cup of chocolate to warm up,' he said.

Dad's drinks tasted great, but nowhere near as rich and creamy and delicious as the hot chocolate Moonface made. Still, poor Dad couldn't really compete with a magic little man who could cast spells, even though he did sometimes muddle them up.

It was getting even colder now, and wisps of

freezing fog hung in the air, giving the Enchanted Wood a really creepy look when they peered out of the window of the cottage. Dad didn't want to drive in the fog, so they couldn't go out for supper anywhere. Mum was full of energy after her nap, so she showed them how to make pizzas, letting them each have a pummel at the dough and choose their own toppings. They weren't quite the same as the pizzas you bought ready-made, but they tasted delicious even so.

It proved to be quite a good day after all, and at least they were all cosy in the cottage now, but the children were still a little anxious, hoping that they'd be able to have another adventure up the Magic Faraway Tree the next day. And the next day and especially on Christmas Day itself.

Birdy was the first to wake up the next morning. She ran to the little latticed window. It was still dark, but there was a strange white glow everywhere, and the windows were silted up with weird white patterns. Birdy stared at them, puzzled. And then she gave a great whoop!

CHAPTER
SEVEN

'MILO! MIA! It's snowed!' Birdy cried, rushing to wake them. 'Let's get up and make a snowman right this minute! No, let's run to the Faraway Tree and make a snowman with Silky and Moonface and Pippin! We could have a snow fight! Or lie down and make snow angels! Quick!'

Birdy had never done any of these lovely traditional things in the snow. It hadn't snowed properly since she was born. But Mum and Dad had read her stories about children playing in the snow, and Granny and Grandad had told her about times when the snow lasted for weeks and all the ponds iced over and they went sledging down big hills on tea trays. Birdy had waited so long for it to snow so that she could play in it too.

She had to wait a little bit longer. Milo was peering through the patterns on his own window.

'That's not snow, Birdy. It's frost!' he said.

'It's beautiful!' said Mia, opening her own window with difficulty and peering right out. It was so cold it made her head ring, but she stayed looking at the magical white world around her. 'It's all glittering!' she said in awe.

'Well, can we make a *frost* snowman?' Birdy asked. 'I mean a frostman. And have a frostball fight? And make frost angels?'

'It's not thick enough to do anything like that,' said Mia.

'But we *could* make a slide!' said Milo.

'What, like the slippery-slip?' Birdy asked.

'What's the slippery-slip?' Mum asked, coming into the room in her dressing gown.

The children shut their mouths and stared at each other anxiously.

'It's . . . it's just a game we play,' Mia said quickly. Well, it was a sort of game, she reasoned to herself, so she wasn't really fibbing.

'Yes, we make out we're going down this slide, round and round,' said Milo, blushing because it sounded as if he played pretend games, and he felt he was far too old to do that.

'Well, you can pretend all you like, kids, but you're not to make a real slide,' said Mum.

'Just in the lane at the back,' said Milo.

'Especially not in the lane, where Dad and I can't keep an eye on you,' Mum said very firmly. 'I know slides are fun, but they're dangerous too. One of you is bound to fall over and break an arm or a leg and I don't want to have to spend all day in hospital while you get it plastered. No slides. Promise?'

They promised reluctantly. Mum wouldn't let them go out before breakfast either. She made them each eat a big bowl of porridge to keep them warm, letting them spoon golden syrup on top.

'Remember when Silky let us spoon syrup and it made lovely pictures all by itself?' Birdy whispered.

She wasn't very good at whispering and Milo and Mia gave her a nudge, but luckily Mum was talking to Dad now and didn't hear. The children waited impatiently until Mum poured a second cup of coffee.

'Can we go and run races in the lane if we promise, promise, promise not to make a slide?' said Milo.

Mum pulled a face. 'It's still very slippery out there. Not today, Milo.'

The children looked devastated.

'Oh, Mum, please. We'll be ever so careful,' Mia promised.

'We absolutely *need* to go and play in the lane,' said Birdy.

'Well, OK, I'll come and keep an eye on you,' said Dad.

'Oh, no, we don't want you to do that!' said Birdy, not very tactfully.

Dad looked crestfallen.

'Oh, Dad! I didn't mean we don't *want* you! It's just . . . just I like being a big girl with Milo and Mia,' said Birdy, rushing to him and throwing her arms round his waist.

'Of course you do, darling,' said Dad. 'OK then. You three go and run your races – but be careful, promise!'

'We'll be *ever* so careful,' said Birdy, and Milo and Mia echoed her.

Mum still didn't want them to go, but she made the best of it. She insisted they put their wellington boots on though, because they had special grippy soles. They didn't really want to climb the Faraway Tree in cumbersome welly boots, but they could see there was no point arguing.

They went out of the back door in all their many winter clothes and the wretched boots. The cold stung their faces and caught their breath, but everywhere looked so strangely beautiful in this silent frosty world that they stood still for several moments instead of running about to keep warm.

Then they ran one lumbering race along the lane just to be able to feel they were telling Mum and Dad the truth. Milo and Mia held hands with Birdy so she couldn't possibly slip on the icy lane. In actual fact it was *so* icy that they very nearly tumbled down together, but they managed to keep their footing somehow and jumped over the ditch into the Enchanted Wood.

It was easier to walk there because the grass was crunchy with frost and they could tramp through it without wobbling. The trees were all like white stone statues, utterly silent and awe-inspiring. They paused, wondering which path to take – but Pippin came racing along, so happy he bounced up and down and then ran a whole circle round them, a great joyful grin on his dear, furry face.

'You'll never ever guess what!' Pippin cried. 'There's the most magical land at the top of the Faraway Tree today!'

'Is it the Land of Christmas?' Milo asked.

'No, not yet, but Silky says it will be coming soon,' said Pippin.

'Great!' said Mia. 'Hey, I wonder if Moonface will dress up as Father Christmas? Wouldn't he look fantastic in a little red robe and a white beard to match his white face?'

'And Silky could be the fairy on top of the Christmas tree!' said Birdy. 'Perhaps I could be a fairy too, with a white dress and wings to match!'

'Sh, you sillies!' said Pippin, giving them each a gentle poke in their ribs. 'It's *my* land!'

'What, the Land of Bears?' Mia asked hopefully. 'After unicorns I think they're my favourite animal.'

'Not just bears. Arctic foxes and oxes – no, oxen – and walruses and whales and reindeer and wolves *and* little brown bears like me, Silky says. Maybe I'll find some friends and relations there, in the Land of the Frozen North,' said Pippin. 'I can't wait! Though I *have* waited so I could come and meet you and take you up there too. You'll need me to protect you!' Pippin said importantly.

'Thank you, Pippin,' said Milo gravely, trying hard to keep a straight face. It seemed so sweet of Pippin to think he could look after them, when he was so little and bumbly and needed constant looking-after himself.

'You're a pal, Pippin,' said Mia, squeezing his paw.

'Can you keep the wolves away, Pippin?' said

Birdy, taking him seriously.

'Easy-peasy! I just give a great big growl like this!' Pippin demonstrated. 'Grrrrrr!'

It sounded mildly fierce, but rather squeaky. Birdy wasn't sure that sort of growl would worry the smallest rabbit, let alone a big bad wolf, but she hoped Silky and Moonface would protect her if there really were packs of wolves in this Land of the Frozen North. Maybe the Saucepan Man would visit it too, and then he could always bash the wolves on their heads with one of his saucepans.

Pippin hurtled forward on all fours, and the children ran helter-skelter behind him. Sometimes they couldn't help sliding on the narrow icy paths, but as they weren't meaning to they hoped they were still keeping their word to Mum and Dad. Many little woodland creatures had made their own slides. Little rabbits and squirrels flew jauntily over the ice, squealing as they went, tiny field mice bowled along, sometimes turning somersaults, and hedgehogs rolled themselves up and whizzed along as if they were balls in a bowling alley. Even birds flew down through the bare branches, perched precariously on their tiny feet, and slid this way and that, flapping their wings for more speed.

The Magic Faraway Tree itself was a thing of beauty, its gnarled old trunk iced all over. It was growing strange red berries that glowed against the white. Birdy reached out to pick one.

'No, don't! It could be deadly poison!' said Milo.

'You mustn't ever eat red berries,' Mia said.

'But they look so pretty. And I eat red raspberries and strawberries, don't I?' said Birdy, but she dropped the berry obediently.

'Come on, up the tree, up the tree to my magic

land!' Pippin urged them, starting to climb, pulling himself up quickly, first his front paws then his back paws in an easy rhythm.

The children found it much harder as the tree was slippery with ice, they were bundled into many winter clothes and their feet were clumsy in their heavy wellington boots. Still, at least it warmed them up, and their cheeks grew almost as red as the berries.

Milo started singing a silly song to urge them along after Pippin.

'*Up* the Faraway Tree, Mia and Birdy and me. *Up* the Faraway Tree!' he chanted.

'That's a rubbish song,' said Mia, but she started singing it too, and Birdy joined in.

They forgot to lower their voices as they passed the Angry Pixie's house. His window was frosted over – but it suddenly flew open and there was the Angry Pixie with a jug of water in his hand. He seemed to have forgotten he might be the Tranquil Pixie now.

'How dare you wake me up!' he shouted, and he tried to fling the water over them. But he had forgotten how cold it was. The water in the jug had frozen solid and stuck fast.

'Sorry we disturbed you, Mr Pixie,' said Milo.

The Angry Pixie shut his window furiously, muttering something.

'Um, he said a very rude word,' said Birdy, giggling. She repeated it herself.

'Stop it, Birdy!' said Mia.

Birdy said it louder, roaring with laughter.

'You don't want Silky to hear you saying that, do you?' said Mia.

Birdy calmed down and climbed quickly, eager to get to Silky's house.

Silky had hung a special Christmas wreath on her door, greenery studded with red holly berries and white mistletoe. Silky herself was looking very Christmassy too, in a green dress with red berries embroidered on the bodice and hem and a white furry jacket with neat holes at the back so that she could still spread her wings.

'Hello, Milo and Mia and Birdy!' she said. 'Well done, Pippin, you found them! My goodness, you look so cold! I think you'd better all have a bowl of porridge before we collect Moonface and go the Land of the Frozen North.'

'We've already had porridge this morning,' said Milo. 'Mum made us have some.' He wasn't very keen on porridge even with golden syrup.

'Though it's very kind of you to offer,' said Mia. She didn't really like porridge either, especially when the lumps took her by surprise.

'And I bet your porridge must be extra awesome,' said Birdy, giving Silky a hug.

'It is!' said Pippin. 'Please may I have some, Silky?'

The children looked surprised, as they knew Pippin was in a tearing hurry to get up to the Land of the Frozen North.

'I'll give you a little bowl each – just three mouthfuls!' said Silky.

She set a big pot on her stove and poured in some ingredients so quickly, they didn't quite see what they were. The pot started bubbling almost immediately. It didn't smell like boring old porridge. It had such a sweet, creamy, wonderful smell that the children's mouths started watering.

'It smells like ice cream!' said Birdy.

'Well it can't possibly *be* ice cream, because that's cold and you can't heat it up, bird-brain,' said Milo, in that rather superior tone that big brothers sometimes take.

'Of course I've got a bird-brain, because I'm Birdy,' she said, and stuck her tongue out at him.

Mia was watching as Silky carefully spooned the porridge into four little blue bowls.

'It *looks* like ice cream, the lovely Whippy sort!' she said excitedly. She dipped the tip of her finger in the bowl nearest her. The porridge was really hot, practically burning her finger, and yet when she put it gingerly in her mouth it really did taste like the best ice cream ever, and so smooth and sweet and creamy that she shut her eyes to savour it properly.

'I think it tastes even better with a little lingonberry sauce,' said Silky. 'I made some early this morning. I was thrilled to see them growing all over the tree.'

'Can you really eat those berries?' asked Milo.

'If you're sure they're real lingonberries,' said Silky. 'You shouldn't eat them raw, as they taste very bitter. But they're lovely cooked, I promise you.'

She poured the beautiful, deep red sauce from a jug. The sauce whirled itself into a beautiful rose shape on top of Mia's bowl.

'Oh, can I have one of those roses on my porridge?' Birdy asked.

Silky poured a rose on to each bowl and handed them to the three children and Pippin. She had fed the little bear two big bowls of porridge already, but she didn't like to leave him out. The sauce was a deliciously sharp contrast to the sweet porridge that in just two minutes the children were scraping their bowls, their insides wonderfully warmed, while their lips were bright red from the lingonberries.

'We look as if we're wearing lipstick!' said Mia.

Milo licked his lips quickly, but they stayed crimson no matter how he tried to wipe them. Moonface laughed when they went up to his little round house.

'Ah! Have you been delving into Silky's make-up bag, Milo?' he said.

'No, I haven't!' Milo said indignantly. 'It's because I've been eating—'

'Lingonberries!' said Moonface. 'I couldn't resist teasing you, Milo, old chap. Lucky you! I'd love Silky to make me a bowl of lingonberry porridge, but nowadays she says I could easily make one for myself. And I haven't got time to faff about cooking – I've got more important things to do!'

'Moonface, you can't possibly say that!' said Mia, appalled.

'I know,' said Moonface, chuckling. 'I was just teasing you too, Mia.'

'Oh, tease me, Moonface!' said Birdy, not wanting to be left out.

'As if I'd tease a little squibbet like you, Birdy!' said Moonface. 'Now, it's very cold outside, and even colder through the clouds in the Land of the Frozen North. I think you need a warmer hat. I'll lend you one of mine.'

He fetched a woolly red hat from his coat hook and set it on Birdy's head. Moonface's head was at least three times the size of Birdy's. The hat came down past her nose, past her chin, and rested on her shoulders, so she couldn't see out in any direction.

'I think it might be a bit too big for me!' Birdy said, her voice muffled by the thick woollen helmet.

'Another little tease!' said Moonface, whipping his hat off her and giving her nose a tiny poke.

'You're in a very jolly mood today, Moonface,' said Milo.

'I think it was because I had such a marvellous holiday in the Land of Sunshine,' said Moonface cheerily. 'It's set me up a treat and restored all my magic powers. Imagine being able to retrieve all our clothes like that, not a garment missing!'

He patted himself on his own back. They were kind enough not to remind him that the clothes had all got totally muddled up during their magical retrieval and it had taken twenty minutes for everyone to swap with everyone else.

'Come *on* please!' Pippin begged, pacing round the room impatiently. 'I can't wait to go up to the Land of the Frozen North! It'll be gone before we get there at this rate!'

'We're coming, we're coming!' said Moonface. 'But just let me give you each a Toffee Shock for the journey.' He handed round his tin of toffees.

They each took one eagerly and started chewing. Then they paused, puzzled. Each Toffee Shock was starting to get warm. They chewed again. It got even warmer as it expanded. It got bigger and bigger, and warmer and warmer. Soon they couldn't talk properly.

'Ooble ooble ot!' Milo spluttered, pointing at his mouth.

'Ooble ooble ot too!' said Mia, fanning herself.

'Ooble ooble aw om!' said Birdy blissfully.

Pippin's mouth was so full, he couldn't say anything at all. He had greedily helped himself to two Toffee Shocks and now he felt like a giant hot-water bottle.

Silky had nibbled her Toffee Shock daintily, but her cheeks were flushing and the tips of her wings were scarlet.

Then all the Toffee Shocks burst simultaneously as they were starting to get almost *too* hot. They were left with a wonderful, warm glow that didn't leave them, even when they stepped outside Moonface's house and started climbing the tree.

Dame Washalot wasn't rub-a-dub dubbing in her tub. Her water had completely iced over, so she couldn't do her washing today. She was inside her house with Dame Ironallday, having a cup of tea and taking it easy. The Saucepan Man and Mr Watzisname weren't in their deckchairs on the big branch near the ladder. They were indoors too, making a terrible noise. The Saucepan Man had taken all his saucepans and kettle off and they were drumming away on them happily with metal spoons.

'Aren't you coming up to the Land of the Frozen North, gentlemen?' Milo called through their window.

'Two men play the drums,
In their fine two-man band.

Who wants to grow numb
In that cold northern land?'

the Saucepan Man sang at the top of his voice, and Mr Watzisname gave a special drum roll on his kettle.

'You could keep warm with one of my winter Toffee Shocks,' Moonface offered, but they weren't tempted.

'Silly old Saucepan Man! Wacky old Mr Watzisname!' said Pippin, rather rudely. 'The Land of the Frozen North must be the best ever land because there are lots of little bears there just like me!'

'Then let's go and find them, little cub,' said Moonface fondly. 'Up the ladder! I'll go first, just to have a peer to make sure it's extra safe.'

'No, *I'll* go first because I'm probably a bit stronger than you,' said Milo. He was quite a bit bigger than Moonface too, but he didn't like to say it.

'*I* should go first because I'm braver than you,' Mia insisted.

'*I* should go first because I'm the only one with wings, so I can fly away quickly from any danger,' said Silky.

Birdy kept quiet because she really, really didn't want to go first. She was still a little worried by the possibility of wolves.

But while they were all arguing Pippin bolted up the ladder before they could stop him and disappeared into the clouds. They heard him give a loud cry – and all scrambled up behind.

CHAPTER EIGHT

PIPPIN STARED in awe at the Land of the Frozen North. His eyes blinked. His little black nose twitched. He clasped his paws in wonder. He was in a land of ice, bright white in the watery sunshine.

The grass was iced over, a forest of tall evergreens frozen solid, creaking in the wind. There was a lake, thick with ice, though a small herd of reindeer had cracked a hole near the edge with their massive antlers and were drinking thirstily. Several big fat walruses had surfaced through another hole in the ice and were lying on their bellies, occasionally raising their heads.

A huge brown bear was squatting by a stream, staring intently through the thinner ice. Then, with a sudden dart of his paw, he grabbed a fish and gobbled it up in an instant.

'Oh my!' Pippin breathed. He leapt off the ladder and hurtled over the icy grass towards the bear. Pippin heard the others calling out to him, telling him to come back, but he took no notice. He slowed down a little as he got nearer the great bear and lowered his head submissively.

'Greetings, great big bear,' Pippin said formally, his voice squeaky with excitement. 'I'm Pippin. I think we might be related. I'm a brown bear too, though only a little cub. Please will you show me how to catch fish like that? It was awesome! That's what my friend Birdy says. She's there, with all my other friends. They look a bit scared of you, but I'm not a bit.'

The great bear sat back on his haunches, finishing off the remains of his fish. Then he bent his great head right down to Pippin, his teeth bared. Pippin shivered, wondering if he was starting to be scared after all. The bear opened his great mouth, raised his huge, powerful arms, and growled.

'Oh, quick, let's rescue poor Pippin!' said Silky, standing on her toes and flapping her wings.

'We're coming, Pippin old chap!' Moonface called, flexing his small fists.

'Pippin! Pippin! Pippin!' Milo and Mia and Birdy cried.

But Pippin was bouncing up and down, grinning all over his face. He started grunting and growling, though his voice was a bit too high-pitched to be threatening. He jumped up and the huge bear leant down so that they touched snouts.

Silky flew to his side and reached out to Pippin, giving the big bear an extremely wide berth.

'Are you all right, darling Pippin?' she asked.

The giant bear growled ferociously, but she stood her ground. Pippin however fell over, lying on his back and kicking his legs in the air.

'Don't cry, Pippin – I'll rescue you!' Moonface panted, running hard and slipping all over the place on the icy grass, his little patent boots unable to get a firm grip. Then he found himself sliding, flailing, flying through the air – and landed with such a bump on his bottom that his eyes started watering.

'Don't you cry, dear Moonface,' said Pippin, spluttering. 'I'm *laughing*! This lovely gentleman relative of mine is so funny!'

The huge bear thumped himself on the chest proudly, grunted again and set Pippin off into further peals of laughter.

The children ran to Moonface, hauled him to his feet, and brushed him down. Mia quickly dried his face with her woolly mitten to preserve his dignity. Then they staggered over to the big bear, though they didn't get too close to him. His teeth looked extremely sharp, and so did his claws.

'Are you *really* speaking bear language?' Milo said to Pippin. 'I didn't know you could do that.'

'Neither did I!' said Pippin, righting himself. 'But as soon as I heard my dear new friend and relative I understood. I can speak it back. Listen!' He grunted again, and this time the big bear laughed, his huge shoulders shaking.

It felt very odd being left out of their conversation entirely. The two bears continued chatting, while the children and Silky and Moonface stood awkwardly, unable to join in.

'Perhaps you could teach us a few words of bear language so we can greet your friend politely?' Silky asked.

'Oh, I don't think *you* could ever speak it,' said Pippin.

Silky flushed. 'I can actually speak quite a few different languages – Elvin, and Gnomish, and Unicornese, and most bird tweets, and my own Fairy of course.'

'Well, go on. Try! Say this!' said Pippin and gave a whole series of grunts that ended in a proper growl.

They'd all heard him grunt and growl before, but they'd never realised that each one had a specific meaning. Silky screwed up her face, concentrating, and then did her best to copy Pippin. She was trying hard, but her grunts were rather snorty, and her growls much too soft.

'Hopeless!' said Pippin, getting totally above himself, strutting around proudly on his back legs. He said something in his new language to the big bear, who nodded, threw back his head and roared so powerfully that Silky quivered, and Moonface and the children put their hands over their ears.

The big bear was obviously calling, summoning someone. Many someones! Bears came running out of the woods – big bears, medium-sized bears, and many baby bears, some even smaller than Pippin. He squeaked excitedly as the bears approached, grunting and thumping himself on the chest. They circled him, all seeming joyous and happy to meet Pippin. Then they looked at Silky and Moonface and the children, and Pippin introduced them, actually saying their names in ordinary speech, but adding little descriptive grunts and growls in bear language.

The big and middle-sized bears all nodded politely, and several of the bear cubs ran up to the children and gave little grunts. The children were enchanted, especially Mia, who sat down on the icy

A CHRISTMAS ADVENTURE

grass and let the bears climb all over her, even though they knocked her woolly hat off and pulled her scarf.

She listened hard as they grunted softly and did her best to grunt back in exactly the same way. That made them jump about, laughing, and give her further grunts. The biggest bear gave her a nod of approval.

'What did I grunt, Pippin?' Mia asked eagerly.

'Just hello,' said Pippin, a little put out that she had learnt to speak a little bear language already. 'All these small cousins of mine said hello, and you said hello back. But you were just copying them.'

'That's the way to learn a language, little chap,' said Moonface. He was digging in the pockets of his voluminous duffle coat and brought out a large paper bag. 'Pippin, ask the big bear if I can give the cubs each one of these!'

Pippin peered in the bag himself. 'Oooh, Toffee Shocks!' he said.

He had a hard time explaining what they were to the big bear. There was no equivalent word for toffee in bear language, and the Big Bear frowned when Pippin said the word 'shock'.

'He thinks it's something nasty,' said Milo.

'Why not say they're ... Honey Surprises?' said Mia.

This was a brilliant suggestion. The big bear took one for himself. He gave a grunt of pleasure as he chewed. Then he chewed again and again, his large jaws working. He stopped, his brown eyes opening wide in surprise.

'There! He gets it now!' said Mia.

Moonface rubbed his hands with glee. 'Wait for it!' he said.

The big bear was trying to grunt, but try as he might, all he could say was, 'Grrooble, grrooble, grooble.' The Toffee Shock expanded enormously, so that the bear shook his head in astonishment. Then it popped at last, and the big bear threw back his head in surprise and delight, drooling down his chin. He clapped his great paws in acknowledgement to Moonface, and nodded enthusiastically at the bag, grunting something to the cubs.

They all capered in front of Moonface, and more came running helter-skelter from the forest.

'Oh, dear, I'm not sure there's going to be enough,' said Moonface.

'Why don't you try a multiplying spell?' said Silky.

'Good idea!' said Moonface. 'So, how does it go?

'Once time is good as gold,
Twice times is worth a fee,
Thrice times is getting bold,
And four times is . . . fiddley dee?'

'Oh, Moonface! It's "clever me",' said Silky.

'But I'm the one who's being clever, not you, Silky!' said Moonface. 'What is that last bit now? Could it be "bumble bee"? Or "riddle-me-ree"? Or "can't you see"?'

'Moonface, I think *you* say "clever me",' said Birdy, pointing at him helpfully.

At last Moonface understood, which was just as well, because he was surrounded by a whole pack of eager cubs trying to snatch the bag from his hand. He repeated the spell:

'Once time is good as gold,
Twice times is worth a fee,
Thrice times is getting bold,
And four times is clever me, clever me, clever me!'

Moonface's paper bag started swelling as the Toffee Shocks increased in number. They soon burst the bag and started bouncing across the ice like little balls. The cubs ran after them, shrieking, trying to grab as many as possible, some stuffing two or even three Toffee Shocks into their mouths.

'No, no, you must only eat one at a time!' said Silky.

Even though they didn't know her language, it was obvious what she was saying, but they were an unruly little pack and took no notice. They started chewing with their sharp teeth. Chewing and chewing and chewing.

'Grrooble grrooble grrooble!' they said happily,

snorting with laughter.

But then the Toffee Shocks popped all at once, with such force that the cubs were blown right off their paws and were thrown on their backs, drooling toffee juice.

'Oh my goodness!' said Silky, darting from one to another, trying to sit them up and pat them on the back.

A little posse of mother bears came running, growling anxiously when they saw their cubs rendered helpless, though they were all giggling feebly. Silky and Moonface tried to explain, and Pippin translated, while Mia grunted 'hello' in bear talk in as friendly a manner as she could manage. The mother bears looked faintly reassured, but each grabbed their own cub and held them in their great furry arms until they recovered.

Pippin watched a little wistfully.

'I don't suppose *I* have a mother here, do I?' he grunted.

The mother bears looked at him kindly, and one picked him up alongside her own cub. She rocked him like a baby while Pippin nestled up to her.

'Could she really be Pippin's mother?' Milo breathed.

'Oh, I do hope so,' said Mia, crossing her fingers.

'I do too – though I hope he can still come and play with us!' said Birdy.

But after a few minutes Pippin started wriggling, trying to free himself from the bear hug. He reached up and gave the kindly mother bear a kiss on her plump cheek, then jumped free.

'Oh, Pippin, darling, you looked so lovely cuddled up to her. *Is* she your mother?' Silky asked softly.

'No, but she says she could still look after me if I want,' said Pippin proudly.

'And *do* you want?' Silky asked.

'Well, a little bit,' said Pippin. 'But that would mean staying here in the Land of the Frozen North and I don't think it's really where I come from. I think I can remember lots of different bears in *my* land – black-and-white panda bears, and spectacled bears, and very slow sloth bears and great big fierce white polar bears and little fluffy red and blue and yellow and green toy bears – they were my special friends...' Pippin drooped a little.

'That sounds like the Land of Bears,' said Moonface brightly, though the others had probably worked that out for themselves. 'I daresay it will come back to the Faraway Tree one day.'

'And meanwhile we'll be your special friends,' said Silky.

'And us too, when we're here on holiday,' said Mia.

'We'll see you every day,' said Milo.

'That will be awesome,' said Birdy. 'And I do hope you'll teach me how to talk like a bear. What's awesome in bear language?'

Pippin tried to puzzle it out. 'I think it's something like "Grrr-g-r-o-w-l",' he said.

'Grrr-g-r-o-w-l!' said Birdy.

All the cubs stared at her and then grinned and laughed. They left their mother bears and scampered round Birdy and Pippin, tumbling about, several of them turning head over heels, intent on showing off. Pippin copied them.

'I can do that too!' said Birdy. She did a rather clumsy roly-poly, but the cubs clapped her nevertheless.

Mia was tempted to join in, but Milo thought he was a bit old for those sorts of antics. Moonface didn't mind looking foolish and turned some somersaults of his own, waving his little legs in the air, making the cubs roll over laughing. Then he started making a slide in the frosty grass, dragging his feet backwards and forwards until he'd made it as slippery as a skating rink.

'It's another slippery-slip!' Moonface declared. 'Look, cubs! This is fun!' He took a run at the slide and slid along it at top speed. They all jumped up to copy him, their paws soon making the slide longer and even more slippery.

Milo and Mia and Birdy watched enviously, longing to have a go themselves, but remembering their solemn promise to Mum and Dad.

'But we only promised not to slide down the lane. We didn't say anything about sliding in the Land of the Frozen North!' said Milo.

'But what if Birdy falls over and breaks an arm or a leg?' said Mia.

'I won't, I promise! And look, the cubs keep falling over and they don't hurt themselves one bit!' said Birdy.

The cubs certainly bounced up again after taking a tumble, laughing even more.

'They're all very plump and padded with fur. Birdy's got little stick arms and legs,' said Mia.

'Oh, all *right*! But it doesn't mean I can't have a go,' said Milo crossly. He marched over to the slide, but his boots slipped every now and then even before he got to it. He wanted to slide so much he didn't care if he broke his own arm or leg – but he did care about his little sister. She would copy him if he went on the slide, even if he told her not to. He knew Mia was right, though it was infuriating to admit it.

He sighed heavily and wandered over to the

lake, where the walruses were lying, flopped on the ice. It looked as if they were sunbathing, though the temperature seemed below zero, and Milo's hands and feet were numb.

'Hello, walruses,' said Milo. 'I wonder if you can understand me? Are you going to have a swim soon? I'm quite a good swimmer, you know. I went swimming with dolphins only yesterday. We all leapt out of the water together and then dived right down. Is that the sort of swimming you do?'

One or two walruses opened their eyes and blinked at him, but they didn't seem very chatty. Milo wondered if he dared try to swim to show them, but when he peeled off his glove and put his hand in the water he practically screamed. He wiped his hand on his coat, shoved his glove back on and nursed it in his armpit, hopping about with pain. He decided swimming in the Land of the Frozen North was definitely a spectator sport.

He saw what looked like an enormous dolphin far out at sea, rising its strange huge head above the waves, and then diving down with an expert flip of its enormous tail.

'Look! Did you see that absolutely gigantic dolphin?' Milo cried, running to his sisters.

'That's not a dolphin, you dope! It's a whale!' said Mia. She remembered the whale page in her giant book about animals back at home. 'I think it's a beluga whale! That's incredible! I never ever thought I'd see one of them.' She peered out to sea, her eyes screwed up against the bright light of the ice.

Birdy was peering in the opposite direction. 'Hey, look, there's a little white dog running about! Oh, it's so fluffy! Here, doggy! Come here, boy!'

Mia turned to look too. 'I don't think it's a dog. It's a fox.'

'No, it's not!' said Birdy. 'Foxes are brown and long and very, very mean.' She had once had a pet rabbit who'd had a terrible encounter with a fox.

'This is an Arctic fox,' said Mia. 'It's lovely!' She moved forward slowly, and then bent down, her arms out, calling to him.

'A fox!' said Silky, looking down worriedly at

her fur jacket. It was fake fur of course, but it didn't seem tactful. She shut her eyes, murmuring something quickly. Her fur jacket suddenly disappeared. She wore a white woollen coat instead, again with neat holes at the back to accommodate her wings.

The little fox approached Mia timidly, and then suddenly ran to her in a rush. She sat right down, not even minding the chill of the ice, and the fox jumped into Mia's arms.

'Ooh!' said everyone.

Mia went bright pink with pride, stuffed her gloves in her pocket and stroked the fox very gently. Its fur was so thick that her hands grew as warm as toast.

'Dear little Arctic fox,' she whispered.

'Can I hold him?' Birdy begged.

'In a minute,' said Mia. 'We can't just hand her from person to person – it will unsettle her.'

'You're just saying that because you're the one holding him,' said Milo. 'And how do you know it's a her anyway? It looks like a little male to me.'

Mia held the fox up for a moment and had a peer. 'Definitely a girl,' she said.

The fox made little snuffling sounds.

'Maybe she's hungry? Shall I give her a Toffee Shock? There are several left,' Moonface asked.

'She's not as robust as the bear cubs. I think your sweets might be too much of a shock!' said Silky. 'She's so little and lovely!' She made a private resolve never ever to wear a fur coat again, even a fake one.

'What do Arctic foxes eat, Mia?' Birdy asked.

Mia screwed up her face. 'I think they eat lemmings,' she said.

'What on earth are they?' said Birdy, puzzled. 'Are they like lemons?'

'They're little rodents – you know, like mice or rats,' said Mia.

'Yuck!' said Birdy. She looked around. 'I can't see any mousey ratty things scrabbling about,' she added thankfully.

'They also eat squirrels,' said Mia.

'Oh, no!' said Moonface, genuinely appalled.

He thought of all his little squirrel friends who visited him every day. He glared at the Arctic fox, who was licking her lips.

'Bad foxy!' he said sternly.

'She can't help her nature,' said Mia. 'And she doesn't just eat meat. Arctic foxes also eat berries.'

'They must be lingonberries then,' said Silky. 'They're the only berries in the Frozen North.'

'I'll see if I can find some in those woods over there,' Milo offered.

He ran over the icy grass, still very swift even in his wellington boots. It felt good to run. The cold had been seeping into his bones. The big reindeer grazing by the frozen lake looked up at him, moving their great heads. Their antlers were very large. Milo wasn't exactly afraid of deer, but he knew it was sensible to be wary. He veered right away from them, leaving the animals to graze in peace, and then made for the wood again.

It was very dark and still under the tall trees. They creaked in the wind, making a very ghostly sound. The ground had completely iced over, so it was like running on thin glass. It cracked and splintered every now and then, so that Milo stumbled and nearly fell. It was very dark too. It would be hard to spot any lingonberry bushes in the gloom. Still, he ran on, not liking to give up now. He wanted to please Silky and show Mia how useful he could be. He was a little bit scared now, but he willed himself to be brave. He was Milo the Magnificent, who had once faced up to fire-breathing dragons. So what if it was as black as night now? He wasn't a little kid any more. He ran on, further and further into the woods, until he was so breathless he had to stop to recover.

He leant against a tree, gasping. He seemed to hear someone else breathing not too far away. He put his hand to his mouth, trying to stop his own breathing for a few seconds. The breathing sound carried on, increasing in volume. Milo stared into the darkness, his heart thumping in his chest. He saw nothing for a few moments – and then two yellow lights shone through the trees. Then two more. Many more.

They were eyes! Milo was staring at a pack of wild wolves!

He turned round and started running in earnest. The wolves gave a sudden terrible howl and started thundering after him. Milo was a very fast runner, the speediest in his whole school, but he knew it would be almost impossible to outrun a pack of wolves. He looked up at the trees, wondering if he could possibly climb to safety, but the tall trunks didn't start branching until way above his head. He couldn't get a grip on those bare trunks, especially when they were coated in frost. Besides, he had to warn the others. He thought of Mia and little Birdy, who was already frightened of wolves. Silky could fly from them, but Moonface was small and spindly and very unlikely to be able to think of any helpful spell when terrified.

Milo kept running, veering to left and right, sometimes circling trees, doing anything to trick the wolves and stop them following him. He thought he'd lost them once, when they all hurtled past and then drew to a halt, sniffing the air and howling furiously, but then the leader caught Milo's scent and they were after him again. Milo ran on desperately, his arms pumping in his puffer jacket, his legs aching in his clumsy wellington boots.

The trees started thinning and he could see the frozen land again, the gleam of the ice and the blue of the sky. He saw the bears cavorting on the slide with Moonface. He saw Silky and Mia and Birdy playing with the Arctic fox.

'RUN!' he yelled as loudly as he could, though he

had hardly any breath left in his body. 'WOLVES!'

Pippin jumped up and down and growled something urgently in bear language – obviously their word for wolves. The adult bears lumbered to their cubs, grabbed them hastily and scattered. The mother bear who had given Pippin a cuddle reached for him too, but he was running towards Silky. The bear grunted something quickly and then scurried away, her own cub clinging to her chest.

'She says we must hurry! The wicked wolves sometimes *eat* little cubs!' Pippin gasped.

Silky clasped one of Pippin's paws and Moonface grabbed the other. Milo and Mia held Birdy. They all started running, but the icy grass was so difficult to race along. Silky spread her wings for extra speed, but it was especially difficult for the children in their wellington boots. The wolves came pounding out of the forest, their huge paws easily gripping the surface.

'The slide, the slide!' Moonface yelled. 'Lengthen the slide so that . . . so that . . .'

'So that we might glide!' Silky shouted.

The icy slide doubled, tripled, quadrupled its length along the grass, right to the tip of the ladder reaching down to the Faraway Tree. The children hesitated for one split second, and then jumped on it. They'd promised Dad not to slide, but this was a serious emergency.

They sped along, almost as if they were flying. The leader wolf tried to leap on to the slide too, but his front paws went one way and his back the other, and he tumbled off, growling furiously. Two more wolves tried, but they couldn't manage it either.

'Hurray!' Milo yelled, pumping his free fist in the air, loving every second of the slide now that they seemed free of danger. The wolves had stopped trying to follow them, and had wheeled round, seeking other prey.

'Not my bear friends!' Pippin squeaked in terror.

But every cub had been scooped up safely, and the adult bears were now climbing the tall trees at the edge of the forest, out of danger.

'Not the little Arctic fox!' Mia cried.

The fox had rushed away at the first cry of wolf, and within seconds her white coat was invisible in the frosty grass. She scampered away safely to hide in her den. The walruses dived leisurely into the lake, away from the danger of being mauled. The beluga whale sailed on serenely, far out at sea.

The reindeer stopped grazing, raising their heavy heads to see the wolves careering towards them, teeth bared.

'Oh, the deer, the deer, the poor deer!' Birdy screamed.

'Don't look! Quick, get down the ladder,' said Milo, trying to protect her.

'No! We have to save them! Make up a spell, Moonface!' Birdy implored.

'Stop the wolves! Save the reindeer!' Moonface gabbled valiantly, but nothing happened.

The reindeer seemed transfixed, not even trying to run, as the wolves got nearer and nearer.

'I don't know any spells about saving reindeer,' Moonface confessed, nearly in tears.

'Run, reindeer!' Mia shouted. 'Please, run

for your lives!'

They all shouted with her, but the reindeer stayed where they were, though they'd started pawing the ground.

'I think they're going to try fighting the wolves,' said Milo.

'But they don't stand a chance – not with those wolf teeth! They'll be ripped apart!' Mia cried, unable to bear it. She put her hands over Birdy's eyes and shut her own.

'Look! Just look!' Milo yelled urgently.

They all looked – and saw each reindeer pawing now as if they were preparing for a massive leap. And then they all rose up in the air, their legs working hard as if they were running. The reindeer soared over the wolves' heads, up and up and up into the sky until they were scarcely visible.

'They're flying!' Silky said. 'Amazing flying! How do they do that without any wings?'

'But deer can't fly!' said Mia.

'Six, seven, *eight* deer!' Milo counted.

'They're not ordinary deer!' Birdy cried. 'They're

reindeer! They're Santa's reindeer!'

'They're flying off to the Land of Christmas!' Moonface shouted, and they all clapped and cheered as the reindeer flew safely away.

CHAPTER NINE

SILKY GAVE the children another mug of her special hot chocolate when they got back so they could recover and warm up a little. Moonface summoned up all his squirrel friends and told them they mustn't go to the Land of the Frozen North and to be sure to avoid anything small and white and furry.

'Plus there are all these wicked wolves!' said Birdy. 'Little Red Riding Hood must have been very brave to talk to one.'

'And very silly to mistake a wolf for her own grandmother!' said Mia. 'I don't think wolves are deliberately wicked. It's just their nature to hunt in packs. They can't help wanting to eat meat. We're going to be eating turkey at Christmas, aren't we?'

'We're not going to rush up to a flock of turkeys and start eating them when they're still alive,' Milo scoffed. '*I* was the one who was very nearly torn limb from limb. Only I outran them, didn't I?'

'And *I* was the one who built the slide and knew the spell to make it even bigger so we could escape!' said Moonface.

Silky and Mia and Birdy rolled their eyes, but couldn't be bothered to argue. Pippin looked up from his mug of hot chocolate, froth all round his mouth.

'I spoke bear language! It's easy-peasy. And I made lots of new friends. But I like my old friends more,' Pippin said, smiling at them all.

They gave him a big hug – and then the children went to Moonface's house and whizzed all the way down his slippery-slip to the trapdoor at the bottom of the tree. Pippin climbed down the outside of the tree, showing off his newly developed bear skills, and then helped the children find the right path home.

*

They were back in the little lane in minutes. They walked the last few steps very slowly, their legs aching dreadfully now, and went through the back door into the cottage. Mum and Dad were on their second cup of coffee. Dad was having a bacon sandwich, munching away happily.

'I'm on holiday!' he said to the children. 'Did you have fun in the lane?'

The children all nodded vigorously as they kicked off their wellington boots and rubbed their feet.

'Can we have a bacon sandwich too?' Milo asked.

'I suppose so. It'll warm you all up,' said Mum, helping Birdy out of her damp winter coat and giving her a cuddle. 'You're freezing, little Birdy!'

'I don't mind,' said Birdy. 'We had such an awesome time in the Land of the Frozen North.'

'In the what?' said Mum.

Milo and Mia were staring at Birdy, horrified. She realised what she'd just said and thought rapidly.

'It's our game,' she said. 'Santa's reindeer are there and they can really fly!'

'Yes, it's our Land of the Frozen North game,' Mia said hurriedly. 'We call it that because it's so cold.'

'And we make out there are wolves there,' said Milo. 'And I help the girls run away from them.'

Dad popped several rashers of bacon in the frying pan and put slices of bread in the toaster.

'I hope you didn't escape these wolves by sliding in the lane?' he said.

'We didn't slide *in the lane*, honestly,' said Mia, which was technically true.

'You're good kids,' said Dad, which made them feel bad. 'Well, Mum and I have thought up a treat for you as we've been a bit fierce. We have to go shopping this morning, and we've discovered there's a pop-up skating rink in the town centre. Let's all go skating together. You guys can have a laugh if *I'm* the one who falls over.'

They felt really guilty then, but it didn't stop them having a great time on the skating rink. Dad *did* fall over, several times, but luckily didn't hurt himself. Milo and Mia clung to the edge at first, wobbly in their hired skating boots, but soon got their balance and managed to swoop round the rink by the end of their session. Birdy was surprisingly good at staying upright, though her skinny legs wobbled this way and that most of the time. It was Mum who proved the really excellent skater, speeding along, sometimes doing a little twirl, and even executing a small jump.

'Wow, Mum! You're brilliant!' said Milo, trying to copy her and falling over.

'I used to go skating every week when I was your age,' said Mum. 'I had a lot of practice. I don't think you're quite ready for jumping yet, Milo – but you're doing brilliantly too. Hang on to my hand and we'll try going really fast, OK?'

Mum took Milo round the rink at speed, then Mia and then Birdy, while Dad clapped at the side. Then Mum gave Dad his own turn, and he managed to stagger round without falling over this time. The children gave him a big clap too.

They bought all kinds of food treats for Christmas, including a big bag of chestnuts which they roasted that evening, after Dad had coaxed a few flames from the wood in the fireplace.

'There's nothing like a proper fire,' Dad said, though the cottage was already warm and cosy now the boiler was working. 'Do you know what we used to do when I was a kid? We wrote letters to Santa telling him what we wanted for Christmas and then sent them up the chimney. Shall we have a go at doing that now, just for a laugh?'

So when they'd eaten their chestnuts Mum tore out a few pages from her notebook and they all wrote down their requests.

'Can they be for whatever we want?' Mia asked.

'Of course,' said Dad.

'Though there's no guarantee Santa Claus will be able to bring you absolutely everything,' said Mum.

'Well, here's hoping,' said Mia. She wrote:

Dear Santa,
Please may I have my own pony? Or a puppy? Or a kitten? Or a guinea pig? Or any kind of animal at all?
Love from Mia

Milo wrote:

Dear Santa,
I'd really love my own game console, though
I know they cost a fortune. And a new pair
of running shoes and a skateboard and an
electric bike even though Mum and Dad say
I'm not allowed.
Cheers!
Milo

Birdy wrote (in big, wobbly print):

Deer Santa,
I want lots of presents but I don't no
wich.
Love Birdy xxx

Mum and Dad joined in too.

A CHRISTMAS ADVENTURE

Mum wrote:

Dear Santa,
Please may I have a new handbag and bottle of
my favourite perfume and beautiful handmade
gifts from Milo, Mia and Birdy?
Love from their mum!

Dad wrote:

Dear Santa,
I'd love a giant Lego set so I can get building with
my children. I'd also be very happy with a new
whittling knife and some hand-drawn cards. No
socks or ties please.
Love from Milo, Mia and Birdy's dad

They read each other's letters with great amusement
and then took turns sending them up the chimney.
Dad held Birdy's hand to make sure she didn't burn
herself and gave her letter an extra flick so that it

flew straight up the chimney and disappeared.

'There, I bet one of Santa's little helpers was flying past and caught your letter to take it straight to the big ho-ho-ho man himself,' Dad said.

'Awesome,' said Birdy.

'It's Christmas Eve tomorrow,' said Mum. 'Poor Santa will be having a very busy day getting all the presents ready. I wonder if there's a Mrs Santa giving him a helping hand?'

'Will he know we're here at the cottage?' Birdy asked, suddenly anxious.

'I'm sure he does,' said Dad. 'And we've got a nice big chimney for him.'

'Won't he get all burnt if he tries to jump down it?' Birdy asked.

'Don't worry, Mum and I always let the fire go right out before we go to bed,' said Dad. 'Now it's time you three went to bed tonight.'

'Will it be snowing tomorrow if it's Christmas Eve?' Birdy asked.

'That would be lovely, but we'll have to wait and see,' said Mum.

'Can I just peep outside the door to make sure it's not snowing already?' Birdy begged.

They all had a quick look – a *very* quick look because it was colder than ever. Everywhere sparkled white in the moonlight – but it was still frost, not snow.

'Oh, dear!' said Dad. 'Let it snow, let it snow, let it snow!'

'Oh, I love that song!' said Birdy. She started

singing it too.

'Dad! Don't get her started! She'll be singing it again and again and again now and driving us all bonkers,' said Milo, but he gave his sister a hug to show he didn't really mind.

'Do you think Silky will come to see me tonight?' Birdy whispered, as the three children went upstairs to bed.

'Maybe not tonight, as it's so freezing cold,' said Mia. 'She'll say goodnight to Moonface, tuck Pippin up in his little bear cave and then hop into bed in her own house.'

'I suppose so,' said Birdy, but she still waited by the window for ages after Mum and Dad had kissed her goodnight and Milo and Mia were fast asleep. Birdy got very cold, though she wrapped her duvet round herself, and she was so sleepy her head kept nodding against the frosty windowpane, but she stayed there, still hoping.

Then there was a little tap at the window and Birdy blinked her eyes and saw Silky hovering right outside. She looked like a little flying snowman in her white wool coat and white woollen hat and white woolly gloves and white boots, though Silky had her own pretty face, not two lumps of coal for eyes and a carrot for a nose.

'Silky! Oh, I *knew* you'd come!' Birdy cried. She couldn't see her properly because of the frost patterns on the window, so she tugged it open.

'I had to make sure you hadn't caught cold after our adventures in the Land of the Frozen North!' said Silky. 'I'm sorry I'm so late! Pippin was still so excited he simply wouldn't go to bed. He just kept running round and round in his pyjamas, turning somersaults, the bad little bear!'

'Will the Land of the Frozen North still be there tomorrow?' Birdy asked.

'I have a feeling it will be a brand-new land,' said Silky.

'You know what it is, don't you?' said Birdy.

'Well, I know what I *think* it will be,' said Silky. 'But you can never quite tell.'

'It won't have any wolves in it, will it?' Birdy wondered.

'I'm pretty sure those wolves are all back in their wood. They're sleeping in their dens and you should be sleeping in your bed. Night-night now!'

'Night-night, Silky! See you tomorrow!' said Birdy.

They blew each other a kiss. Then Silky flew away, waving her white woolly glove, and Birdy closed the window and jumped into bed, pulling the duvet right up over her head. If Milo and Mia had been awake, they might have heard a muffled, 'Let it snow, let it snow, let it snow!' before Birdy fell asleep too.

She woke up early, gave her toy dog Gilbert his usual good-morning hug and jumped out of bed. She ran to the window and looked out. It was still dark, but enough moon was left to show her a new white world. It had really snowed in the night, just as she'd hoped! This wasn't the strange, spiky world of sharp frost. This was a soft, silent world of thick snow, which blanketed the little cottage garden, rethatched the roof and clung to the bare branches of the trees in the Enchanted Wood.

She leapt out of bed and ran to wake Milo and Mia.

'It's snowed, it's snowed, it's snowed!' Birdy shouted.

'Oh, Birdy, it's not snow, it's frost,' Milo muttered, the pillow over his head.

'Sh, Birdy, it's way too early to get up! Go back to bed,' Mia mumbled, burrowing deep down under her duvet.

'No, you two get up! Let's go out and play! I want to build a snowman and lie on my back and make a snow angel and have a snow fight like children do in books! Come on, wake up! Wake up!' Birdy cried, tugging at their duvets.

They both sat up, protesting. Then they realised there was a strange silence outside and an eerie pale light. Milo grabbed his torch, Mia ran to the window – and they cried out too.

'See!' Birdy said. 'Isn't it awesome?'

'Oh, it's absolutely awesome!' said Milo.

'It couldn't be more awesome if it tried!' said Mia.

'Let's get dressed and go outside and play in it!' said Birdy.

They pulled on as many jumpers and socks and jeans and coats and woolly hats and gloves as they could manage, and then crept downstairs as quietly as they could. Their wellington boots were lined up by the door, ready and waiting. They stepped into them, undid the bolt of the back door and ran out into the garden.

It was still dark, but the moon shone down on the thick white snow. Milo didn't even need to switch on his torch.

'Ooh!' cried Birdy, jumping about joyously, the snow above her ankles.

'Sh!' Mia whispered. 'You'll wake Mum and Dad and they'll send us back to bed!'

'We have to be as quiet as mice,' said Milo, busy making his very first snowball.

Mia saw what he was doing. She clasped a handful of snow, patted it quickly into shape and they threw simultaneously. Milo managed to get her on the shoulder. Mia knocked his woolly hat sideways.

They both cried out.

'Um, that's not as quiet as mice, you two!' said Birdy. She threw a snowball too, but her arms were so bound up in jumpers and her coat she couldn't aim properly. She gave up and lay flat on her back and flapped her arms up and down in the snow.

'Birdy, you're getting all wet!' said Milo, pelting his sisters with more snowballs.

'I'm making a snow angel!' said Birdy. She struggled up again, hampered by all her winter clothes, and jumped clear. There was her snow angel imprinted in the snow, with distinct wings, though perhaps they weren't as delicate as Silky's.

'I'm going to make one too,' said Mia, lying down.

'Well, *I'm* going to make a snowman,' said Milo. He knelt down and started piling up the snow as best he could, though he hadn't bothered to put on any gloves and the cold made his hands ache.

'What you need is a shovel,' said Mia, lying on her back and flapping her arms.

'Aha!' said Milo, and went to look in the garden shed. He found an old garden spade, a little too big for him to handle comfortably, but he set to work determinedly. 'I'm going to make the biggest snowman ever,' Milo said, panting as he shovelled.

'Well, I'll make the biggest snow-woman ever!' said Mia, jumping up and smiling at her own snow angel.

'Well, I'm going to make the biggest snow-baby ever!' said Birdy, kneeling down and trying to mould the snow like Plasticine. She didn't quite have the knack and her snow-baby kept falling to bits. She was feeling very damp, though she tried not to mind.

Mia noticed. 'I think you'd better go indoors and take all those wet clothes off, Birdy,' she said. 'You're shivering.'

'No, I'm not! I'm . . . I'm trembling with excitement because it's snowed at last!' Birdy insisted.

'Tell you what, let's go in the lane and have a proper race to warm up,' said Milo, who was finding making a giant snowman harder than he'd imagined.

'OK,' said Mia. Her hands were stinging with the cold even though she was wearing her woolly gloves. She clapped them together to try to warm them up.

They crunched their way through the snow to the garden gate, though they had a hard job opening it because it had so much snow on either side. In the end Mia vaulted over, Milo hauled Birdy up into Mia's arms and then jumped over himself. They started running down the lane, though the snow was even thicker there. They lumbered along, all three looking at the ditch that divided them from the Enchanted Wood.

It looked beautiful in the snow – more magical than ever.

'Shall we just go in and have a quick peep at the Faraway Tree?' said Mia.

'Well, we *could* – but what if Mum and Dad wake

up early and we've gone missing?' said Milo.

'Time stands still when we're there – you know that,' said Mia.

'Yes, but they'd see our footprints in the garden,' said Milo. 'Perhaps we'd better wait till after breakfast. I'm starving anyway.'

'Silky could make us some breakfast – something really yummy,' said Birdy. 'Let's go and see her!'

'Yes, but how would we explain away the footprints?' Milo insisted.

'Don't be so boring, Milo,' said Mia. 'Come on, Birdy. We'll go, shall we?'

Milo was furious when they held hands and jumped over the ditch. How dare Mia call him boring when he was just being sensible and didn't want to worry Mum and Dad? He picked up a scoop of snow and threw it hard at Mia's head. He wanted to knock *her* woolly hat right off and he succeeded. But Mia clutched her head and doubled up.

'Oh, Mia!' said Birdy, sounding horrified. 'You poor thing! Milo, you're so mean – you've really hurt her!'

'No, I haven't. Mia threw a snowball at *my* head and it didn't hurt a bit. She's just pretending to make me feel bad!' Milo protested. He did feel bad actually. Maybe Mia really was hurt. She didn't usually make a fuss when they were having a mock fight.

He had to jump over the ditch too and see if she was all right.

'Mia?' Milo touched her tentatively on the shoulder. 'Here, let me look at your head.'

He gently lifted her hand out of the way and saw the reddening bump on her forehead.

'Oh, I'm so sorry! I really didn't mean to hurt you. It was just meant to be a joke,' Milo said.

'Yes, well, it wasn't very funny,' said Mia huffily. Her eyes were watery and it was obvious she was trying not to cry, which made Milo feel worse.

He bent to pick up her hat and put it back carefully on her head, covering up the bump. Then he gave her an awkward hug.

'Sorry, sorry, sorry, sis,' Milo muttered. 'Look, tell you what. You make a really hard snowball and chuck it at me. I promise not to duck. Then you'll have got your own back.'

'What's the point of that?' said Mia, sniffling.

'I bet Silky has some magic ointment that makes bumps better,' said Birdy. 'Let's go and find her.'

But now it was Mia's turn to hang back.

'Maybe we shouldn't go any further,' she said. 'I think you were actually right about the footsteps in the garden, Milo. If Mum or Dad look out of their window, they'll see them and go looking for us. Even if we appear back in the garden right away, they might see our footsteps along the lane too, right over the ditch into the Enchanted Wood, and then they'll go bananas.'

'But now we've done it we might as well carry on,' said Milo.

'You two! You keep changing your minds!' said Birdy. 'Let's go and see Silky please!'

So they walked on towards the Magic Faraway Tree.

CHAPTER
TEN

THE WOOD was bustling with little creatures enjoying the novelty of the snow. Rabbits and mice and voles scampered across the paths making criss-cross patterns with their paws. Squirrels darted up and down the trees, throwing tiny snowballs at each other, and the birds flew up in the air, singing even though it wasn't yet dawn.

The children heard happy little grunts in the distance.

'Pippin!' said Birdy.

He came scurrying through the snow towards them. Pippin had clearly been playing roly-poly because he looked like a little white polar bear instead of a brown cub. They all gave him a hug.

'Shall I show you how to make a snow angel, Pippin?' Birdy said excitedly, throwing herself on her back.

'Birdy! You're already soaking wet!' said Mia.

'Then it doesn't matter, does it?' said Birdy, flapping her arms to make the imprint of wings in the snow, then jumping up to show Pippin.

He copied her, waving his paws about so vigorously that he created his own little snowstorm.

'Now *you're* soaking wet too, Pippin – and so are we!' said Mia, brushing her coat.

'But we can get dry if we just shoogle and shake,' said Pippin. He stood and danced up and down, pumping his arms and pounding his legs, and all the snow flew off him, leaving his fur barely damp.

Birdy tried copying him, shoogling and shaking so vigorously she fell over, which made her even wetter.

'We can't do it, Birdy,' said Mia. 'Pippin has the sort of fur that doesn't absorb water.'

'Well, you're really lucky, Pippin,' said Milo,

who was so sodden by now that his coat felt as heavy as lead. 'Hey, we can be really cheeky to the Angry Pixie and we won't care a bit when he chucks a jug of water at us. We can just shake it back at him. Come on, let's try it!'

The three children and the little bear scurried along to the Magic Faraway Tree and started climbing. Pippin reached the Angry Pixie's window first. He tapped on the window with his paw.

'Yoo-hoo, Mr Pixie! Draw your curtains and look at me!' Pippin called, pulling a funny face.

But the curtains remained shut. When Milo came up the tree he read the little notice stuck on the Angry Pixie's door.

It said, 'Away on a visit!'

'I wonder where he's gone? Oh well, never mind,' Milo said.

Pippin looked disappointed.

'That's a shame – I *so* wanted to play the trick on him,' he said. 'Hey, shall I do it to Silky instead?'

'But Silky doesn't throw jugs of water at you, does she?' said Milo.

'No, Silky's always lovely to me. But maybe I could *ask* her to do it!' said Pippin.

'That would be a bit weird,' said Milo, but Pippin wouldn't be deterred.

He scrambled upwards until he got to Silky's daffodil-yellow front door. He peered in her window. Her curtains were open already. He spotted her busy slicing bread on her kitchen table.

'Hey, Silky! Come and throw a jug of water at me!' Pippin cried excitedly, tapping at her window.

'Hello, Pippin! Happy Christmas Eve,' Silky called, not even looking round.

'I'm being cheeky and annoying you, see?' said Pippin. 'So you have to come and open your window and throw a jug of water at me!' He was chuckling so much he could hardly get his words out.

'Oh, I do, do I?' said Silky, not pausing in her slicing. 'All right then. Window, open up please.'

The window flew open of its own accord.

'Jug, empty yourself all over Pippin,' said Silky.

She had a big decorative jug of holly branches in the middle of her table. The jug grew sturdy feet, waddled to the window and thrust itself forward. All its water came pouring out – along with the branches of holly, which gave Pippin little prickly thwacks.

'Ow! Ouch! Stop them, Silky!' Pippin shouted. He shook himself too, but in the wrong direction. Milo got drenched – and received several prickly thwacks himself.

'Silky! Stop it!' Milo begged.

'Stop it *please*?' Silky suggested.

'Please!' Pippin and Milo said in unison.

'Of course, boys,' said Silky. She gave the holly branches a glance and they immediately darted back into the jug, which waddled over to Silky on its stumpy feet. She refilled it with water – and then held it up enquiringly.

'Would you like to play this game again, Pippin?' she asked.

'No thank you!' he squeaked.

'That's sensible,' said Silky, and put the jug on the table.

Mia and Birdy were watching wide-eyed. Silky

was always so sweet and kind. It was unlike her to play a trick on anyone. She was looking particularly fairy-like today too, in a pale-pink flouncy dress, with pink and white rosebuds in her hair. Her wings were pink and white too, and looking extra feathery.

'How come you have roses in your hair, Silky, when it's the middle of winter?' Mia asked.

'Because I'm magic,' said Silky, smiling.

'And how did you make the holly branches jump about like that?' asked Birdy. 'Could you teach me how to do it too?'

'I wish I could, Birdy, but it's not really something you can learn. Dear Moonface went to Enchanter School for many years, but he still gets rather muddled at times. My own magical powers come and go. They seem especially strong at Christmas time, which is a special little present just for me!'

'Not for the rest of us!' said Milo, dripping all over the place.

'I'm so sorry, Milo. Do come in and sit by the fire to get dry. Please, all of you,' said Silky.

'Can I come in too?' Pippin murmured hopefully.

'Of course you can, darling. But give yourself a big shake outside first,' said Silky.

She quickly whispered to the children that Pippin had been very bouncy and boisterous yesterday, showing off his new bear language and frightening the littlest squirrels with his growls. He'd done so many roly-polys that he'd accidentally knocked the Saucepan Man right out of his deckchair and sent him tumbling down the tree with such a clang and clatter of pans that everyone had rushed out of their homes in terror, convinced they were under attack.

Mr Watzisname had thrown himself headlong down the tree in a desperate attempt to rescue his dear friend. He had ended up black and blue with bruises, though the Saucepan Man himself had been protected by his armour of pans and kettles and had landed unscathed.

'They're now in bed recovering, being tenderly nursed by the Angry Pixie, bless him,' said Silky. 'It's very touching. Now gather round the fire, everyone. You'll soon get your clothes dry – and you can make yourselves toast at the same time.'

She brought out four big toasting forks from a cutlery drawer, stuck a slice of bread on each one and showed them how to hold the toast at just the right angle so that the slices turned golden brown. Pippin was a little too eager and his first slice of toast was burnt to a crisp, but Silky knew he hadn't done it on purpose so she gave him another slice of bread to try again.

She gave each of them a plate. They looked like plain white plates, but when Milo studied his he saw it had a large red dragon standing on its hind legs. Mia's plate had a multicoloured unicorn with a long silver horn. Birdy's had a fairy design – a flock of tiny Silky lookalikes. Pippin had little brown bear cubs gambolling round the edge of his plate.

Silky handed them a dish of butter next. They didn't need knives. Pats of butter leapt on to each piece of toast and spread themselves smoothly. Then she brought a pot from her larder with a spoon. Milo helped himself.

'Oh, yum, chocolate spread, my favourite!' he said.

'No, it's apricot jam, *my* favourite!' said Mia.

'No, it's strawberry. Awesome!' said Birdy.

'It's honey, honey, honey!' said Pippin, trying to cram his entire piece of toast into his mouth.

Silky gave them all the same drink – her very special hot chocolate with whipped cream. They ate and drank in blissful silence, and by the time they finished they were as warm as their own toast, and their clothes were completely dry.

Moonface came calling and he was given a cup of hot chocolate too, and several slices of toast with butter and marmalade. (He didn't tell Silky that he'd just finished his own breakfast of egg, bacon, sausages, tomatoes, hash browns and baked beans.) Silky's clock on her mantelpiece guessed this and changed its steady tick to, 'Greedy guts, greedy guts, greedy guts,' with both its hands pointing straight at Moonface.

'It's so cold, you need to eat well to warm yourself up,' Moonface said defensively, as he unbuttoned his very tight waistcoat.

Silky nibbled her own slice of toast with lemon curd and smiled fondly at her friend.

'Then you must feel absolutely boiling hot, Moonface,' she murmured, but he just grinned.

'That was so lovely, Silky. Thank you! But now can we go up the ladder to see what land is at the top today?' Mia begged. 'Do you think the Land of Unicorns might possibly be back?'

'No, I want to dance with my little prince in the Land of Princes and Princesses! That would be awesome!' said Birdy.

'I'd like the Land of Dragons to come back!' said Milo, though he'd had such a terrifying experience there that he still sometimes had nightmares about it.

'The Land of Bears, the Land of Bears, the Land of Bears!' Pippin demanded, bouncing up and down and nearly knocking the table over.

'Well, we'll just have to see,' said Silky, dressing herself in a fluffy pink coat and putting a big pink and white hat on her head like a giant marshmallow.

Moonface shrugged on his duffle coat and wrapped his very long scarf at least twenty times round his neck, until his big white face was scarcely visible.

The children put on all their outdoor things too, and Pippin fluffed up his fur.

They were ready! It seemed colder than ever as they left Silky's cosy house. She was having difficulty closing her yellow door. Something seemed to be stuck at the bottom of it. She bent to look closer. Her funny clock had scampered after them and was trying to get out of the door too, with one little foot wedged tight.

'Do you want to come to the magic land too, clock?' Silky asked.

'Tick tock, yes please, tick tock, yes please!' said the clock.

'Very well – but only if you put on the little hat and the mittens I knitted for you,' said Silky.

Silky's clock struck twelve with excitement,

and soon looked adorable in its red woolly hat and mittens. Silky offered to carry the clock up the tree as its legs were so small, but the clock insisted on climbing in its own way, going round and round the tree.

'It's going clockwise!' said Milo, chuckling.

They went past Dame Washalot and Dame Ironallday's little cottage. Steam hissed out of their window as they'd had to hang all the laundry inside to stop it freezing on the washing line.

'Do you want to come and see which magic land it is today, dames?' Mia called.

'We're too busy!' they replied. 'Everyone wants spotlessly clean, carefully ironed clothes to wear on Christmas Day!'

The Saucepan Man and Mr Watzisname were still in their beds recovering from their spectacular fall. The Angry Pixie was busy making them cups of tea and refilling their hot-water bottles.

'I suppose you're not up to visiting the new land at the top of the tree, gentlemen?' Moonface asked, peering through their window.

'Sadly not, as you can see,' said Mr Watzisname.

The Saucepan Man still had his eyes shut, but managed to sing weakly:

'Two old men are poorly,
A friend rushed off his feet,
A magic land that is surely
A fine seasonal treat!'

'Aha! That's me! The friend rushed off his feet!' said the Angry Pixie proudly.

'A very dear, kind friend,' Mr Watzisname said gratefully, sipping his tea.

'What would we do without you, dear chap?' the Saucepan Man murmured, and started snoring softly.

'Sh now!' the Angry Pixie said to the children, putting his finger to his lips. 'Let the poor man have a rest!'

They nodded obediently and climbed a little further up the tree, until they were nearly at the foot of the ladder that led to the magic land above the clouds.

'What did the Saucepan Man mean by "a fine seasonal treat"?' Mia wondered.

'I know!' said Milo. 'I bet you anything it's snowing up there too, and there'll be snowmen – you know, ones that can walk and talk!'

'That would be awesome!' said Birdy. 'I love the snowman in my book!'

'It wouldn't be awesome at all!' said Moonface, turning even paler than usual. 'Remember the Land of Ice and Snow, Silky?'

'When there was a terrible battle between the snowman and the polar bears?' said Silky.

'Oh, wow! I'd love to see that,' said Milo.

'I'd love to see polar bears!' said Mia.

'I could talk polar bear language, I'm sure I could,' said Pippin.

'But I'm not sure I like battles,' said Birdy.

'Quite right too,' said Moonface. 'That one was very fierce too. And the snowman was very scary.'

'Who could be scared of a snowman?' said Milo. 'All you have to do is throw a big snowball and knock his head right off!'

'I don't think it's the Land of Ice and Snow,' said Silky. 'The Saucepan Man wouldn't say that would be a treat. So, let's think what's seasonal.'

'What exactly does "seasonal" mean?' Birdy asked.

'It's to do with this time of year,' Mia explained.

'Well, that's easy-peasy!' said Birdy. 'It's very nearly Christmas! It's Santa!' She jumped up and down so excitedly, she very nearly fell right out of the tree.

'I don't think it's Santa just yet,' said Silky. 'Shall I fly up and have a peep just to make sure it's safe?'

Silky's clock started ticking very loudly and stamping its small feet.

'It doesn't want you to go!' said Milo.

'Neither do I!' said Moonface. 'I shall go first. You stand back, Silky!'

'Oh, you two!' said Silky fondly. 'I shall be perfectly safe.' She picked her clock up and patted its anxious little face. 'Don't worry. I'll be back in a tick!'

'Tock!' said the clock. 'Tick tock, tick tock, tick tock!'

'Well, I shall grip your ankles fast,' said

Moonface. 'Just shout if you see any snowmen and I'll yank you back down!'

Silky flew up the ladder, not bothering to touch any of the rungs.

'Oh, I wish *I* could fly!' said Birdy.

They heard Silky give a little gasp – but it was one of joy, not fear. Moonface pulled her down all the same, just to make sure. He tugged so hard that Silky came down in a rush, almost on top of him.

'Gently, Moonface,' said Silky, laughing. 'Don't worry! There aren't any snowmen up there, I promise. Come on up, everyone. It's the Land of Toys!'

CHAPTER ELEVEN

THEY ALL raced up the ladder and arrived in the most extraordinary land. It was like a vast airport, with screens everywhere and people bustling about on many different levels – but it was beautiful! The ceiling was completely covered in twinkling fairy lights and paper chains and tinsel and hanging glass bells that tinkled softly overhead. There were vast decorated Christmas trees that filled the huge complex with their delicious fresh pine scent. It mingled with the smell of fruit punch and hot chocolate and cinnamon buns and mince pies available on little stalls where you could help yourself.

Elves in bright green costumes skipped happily up and down the aisles pushing huge trolleys containing beautifully wrapped presents tied with satin bows, all carefully labelled. A senior elf with a clipboard and impressive cap with bells came up to the Faraway Tree visitors with a welcoming smile.

'Welcome to the Land of Toys!' he said. 'I am Sweetmeat, Santa's number-one helper. Is it your first time here? If you consult the screens, you will see which floor and bay you can find your particular interests. The toy workshops are all on the left-hand side – traditional, cuddly, construction, electronic and transport. Then there's packaging and despatch to the right, and the adjoining stables for the reindeer.'

'Oh, let's go and see the reindeer!' Mia cried.

'No, let's go to electronic toys!' Milo said.

'Could we see the cuddly toys first?' Birdy begged.

'Are there cuddly *bears*?' Pippin wondered.

'Do you think there are toy trains?' Moonface asked eagerly.

'I'd love to see if there are any fairy dolls that go on the top of Christmas trees,' said Silky.

Silky's clock danced up and down, ticking loudly and pointing to itself.

'You want to see if there are any toy clocks, don't you?' said Silky, giving it a fond pat.

Sweetmeat smiled at them all.

'Then I suggest you do a grand tour, taking in everything. There's an introductory room on the left of the ground floor. I should start there,' he said.

'But that means we won't get to the reindeer till last and maybe they'll have flown away with Santa by the time we get there!' said Mia.

'I promise you that they won't be setting off until dusk,' said Sweetmeat. 'They'll be sleeping now, building up their strength. If you work your way around at your leisure, you'll arrive at the stables at feeding time, and that will be much more interesting.' He checked the big pocket watch in his elf jacket. 'Please excuse me. I have a million things to check. As you can imagine Christmas Eve is our busiest day of the year.'

He skipped off, the bells on his cap jingling merrily.

'I love the way all the elves are skipping! Can we skip too?' Birdy asked.

'If you want to,' said Silky, smiling.

Birdy skipped down the corridor to the introduction room, holding hands with Pippin. Silky skipped after them, holding her skirts out daintily and pointing her toes. Silky's clock bounced along after her, chiming at every step. Moonface danced a weird kind of jig behind them.

Mia and Milo looked at each other. They agreed that it was a bit strange for children their age to charge about skipping. But it did look fun. They took one step, skipped the next and were soon leaping about, barging into each other deliberately and roaring with laughter.

They thought the introductory room might be a bit boring, with leaflets explaining the detailed history of toy making and a map of the entire complex with 'You Are Here!' in red in one corner. It was a surprise. The room was in semi-darkness, only lit by fairy lights. Everyone sat down on velvet seats. Pippin took his time, jumping from one seat to another, until Silky grabbed him and sat him down beside her.

'Ho, ho, ho!' said a jolly voice – and a very familiar image flashed on to a large screen in front of them. It was of a delightful portly gentleman with white hair and beard, a rosy jolly face and blue twinkling eyes. He wore a long red gown edged with white. There was only one man in the whole world who dressed like that.

'Santa!' Birdy cried out excitedly.

'That's right, Birdy!' he said, which gave everyone a big surprise, because he wasn't there in person, he was appearing on a screen – and how did he know who Birdy was?

'I've got many names. I'm Santa Claus, Father Christmas, Saint Nicholas, Kris Kringle, Père Noël . . . but I'm one and the same person, the funny old gentleman who brings children toys at Christmas time. They're all made here at my special toy factory. We work hard all year – but Christmas Eve is our busiest time! My dear elves are trying their best to make last-minute requests, parcel them all up and get them ready for delivery tonight. It will be a challenge to reach everyone by dawn on Christmas Day, but I have a splendid set of reindeer – fresh and vigorous and fine flyers.'

The children nudged each other. They knew where the reindeer came from!

'I think my dear chief elf, Sweetmeat, has already told you to feel free to wander around and see for yourselves the variety of our toys. Birdy, maybe you will spot a special something that you particularly like as you weren't quite sure what you wanted. Milo and Mia, I do hope you will be pleased with your own Christmas presents. And you, Silky and Moonface.'

Pippin bounced in his seat a little anxiously.

'And I've got something really special for you, Pippin!' said Santa.

Pippin clapped his paws and kicked his legs in the air.

'Enjoy your time here, my dears. Take refreshments whenever you feel in need. I must go and prepare for my big night. I wish you a very merry Christmas!'

The image on the screen faded.

'Wow!' said Milo. 'It was actually *him*, wasn't it?'

'Yep, we've been talking to the real Santa!' said Mia.

'And he knows my name!' said Birdy.

The screen showed a Christmas tree with decorations and lots of brightly wrapped presents. 'We Wish You a Merry Christmas' started playing.

'Oh, no!' Milo groaned. 'It's going to set Birdy off again!'

'Let's sing it too, just this once,' said Mia.

Silky and Moonface and Pippin didn't know the song, but it was easy to learn the words. They all sang it together, and when they came out of the introductory room they heard the elves singing it as they skipped all over the huge Christmas complex.

The six visitors sang as they went up the stairs to the traditional toy department. It was decorated with great swathes of holly and mistletoe, with a beautiful Christmas tree in each aisle hung with glass baubles and gingerbread men and candy canes, with fairy dolls on the top of each one.

'Fairies!' said Silky.

'Gingerbread men!' said Moonface. 'I haven't tasted one of those for ages!'

'Ah! My gingerbread men are fully edible,' said a very elderly lady elf. 'I don't like to boast, but everyone says they are utterly delicious. Would you like to try one, young man?' The elf had her own gingerbread kitchen and was busy icing hundreds of ginger people. She looked a little like a ginger person herself, with two twinkly black eyes like currants in her smiley face.

Moonface preened at being called a young man.

'Yes please, madam elf!' he said.

She selected a gingerbread man who had a very big head and rather spindly arms and legs. It looked uncannily like Moonface, especially when she iced his head bright white. She took other icing bags and piped him a smart red jacket and green trousers.

'Here you are, my dear,' she said, handing the gingerbread man to Moonface. He held him very carefully, pulling a funny face.

'I don't know what to do!' he said. 'He smells delicious! My mouth's watering! Yet he looks so splendid I don't like to eat him. I think I have to keep him.'

'Bless you, dear, but it's his destiny to be eaten. Go on now, gobble him up!' the elf encouraged Moonface.

'Well, perhaps I'll just have a little nibble at one of his feet,' said Moonface. He took a tiny bite – and then another and another and another. He couldn't help himself. He started bolting him down until the gingerbread man had entirely disappeared, apart from a smear of icing on Moonface's cheek.

'Oh, bliss!' he said dreamily.

'Please could we have one too, madam elf?' said Milo. He'd never called anyone madam before and it sounded funny, but he wanted to be polite.

'Of course you can, my boy,' she said. She cast her eye over Mia and Birdy. 'And I dare say you'd like one too, little girls?'

She gave Milo a gingerbread boy with legs and Mia and Birdy each a gingerbread girl with a long skirt.

'Ha, mine's got proper legs so he can run around,' said Milo, making his gingerbread boy leap about.

'But ours have got wide skirts, so we get much more gingerbread,' said Mia. She had never willingly worn a skirt in her life, but for once she was pleased, though she nibbled each side of the skirt first to give her gingerbread girl a pair of jeans.

'My gingerbread girl is a princess because her dress is extra-long and she's got silver balls on her head like a tiara!' said Birdy. 'Awesome!'

Pippin was jumping up and down enviously. 'Do you happen to have any gingerbread bears, madam elf?' he asked.

'Of course,' she said, and handed him a tubby gingerbread bear with a big smile showing iced white teeth.

'Oh, yum!' said Pippin, eating him up in three big bites.

Silky's clock was jumping up and down too, tick-tocking excitedly, determined not to be left out. The elf lady handed it a totally circular gingerbread biscuit with figures iced all the way round and two hands pointing upwards to twelve. Silky's clock ate it eagerly and then chimed twelve noon and then twelve midnight until they were nearly deafened.

'And what about you, pretty fairy girl?' the gingerbread elf asked.

'I'd like a little gingerbread biscuit please, madam elf,' Silky asked. She always had a rather small appetite.

'Of course!' the elf replied and handed her a tiny gingerbread fairy with rainbow sprinkles on its wings.

Silky ate her slowly with little licks and nibbles, absolutely enchanted.

Then they wandered round the traditional department, watching as a hundred elves sat at benches making toys. There were hoops and spinning tops and dolls' prams and toddlers' trikes and bouncy balls of all different sizes. An elf was blowing glass over a flame, making beautiful marbles with red and green and yellow swirls.

Milo loved the woodwork benches most of all. Some of the elderly elves were whittling wood just the way Dad did, whistling as they worked, making funny little toys, wooden chicks that pecked at the painted grass and wooden dogs that wagged their tails. There was even a wooden bear cub that turned head over heels just like Pippin.

'Would you like to try your hand, laddie?' an elf asked Milo.

'Well, I'm not very good at it,' said Milo. 'But I'd love to have a go!'

He sat beside the elf, took a sharp knife and a thick wooden stick and started whittling. Dad had already taught Milo how to hold the knife safely and make a start. He blocked out a basic shape, trying to make a simple little doll for Birdy, but he accidently made the head almost as big as the body.

A CHRISTMAS ADVENTURE

'Is that *me*?' Moonface asked, sounding thrilled.

'Yes, it is,' said Milo quickly. He went on whittling while the others wandered round the wooden toy area.

Mia loved the rocking horses with long manes and tails and real leather saddles. She was allowed to sit on several, trying them out for comfort and rockability. It wasn't as exciting as riding real horses, but she still liked them very much.

Birdy was fascinated with the doll's houses. Some were very big and grand, roofed with real tiny tiles. They had latticed windows and proper front doors with miniature knockers in the shape of lions' heads. Some came fully furnished with sofas and beds and little baths and lavatories, while others were empty, waiting for a child to design their own interiors. Birdy pretended her fingers were a tiny person and walked them in and out of the rooms.

Pippin loved the Noah's arks, especially the one being painted as he watched. He liked the big splosh of red paint for the roof, the blue waves around the edge of the ark and all the varied colours of the animals. He nibbled his lips as he watched the elf paint tiny dots on the two giraffes and black and white stripes on a pair of zebras. Pippin marvelled at the tiny scales painted on the bright green snakes. Then he held his breath as the elf picked up a pair of wooden bears. Was he going to paint them white and make them polar bears? Or would they be fierce golden bears? No, they were little brown bears, and Pippin clapped his paws.

Silky's clock stumped around trying to peer at everything. It was too little to see the work benches properly, but Silky kindly picked it up so that it could have a proper view. It took a mild interest in everything, but then was particularly amused by the wooden cuckoo clocks. An elf was busy inserting little wooden birds into the clocks and testing their cuckoos as they burst out of their hidey-holes. The first took Silky's clock by surprise and it hiccupped a whole series of tick-tick-ticks in astonishment. The second made Silky's clock shake with laughter, and the third made it chime in unison. It grew very noisy, but Silky had to stay there for a good ten minutes, it was having such fun.

Silky was very taken with a wonderfully carved musical box covered in an intricate design of flowers.

'Perhaps you'd care to wind the handle for me?' the elf making it offered, thrilled that a real fairy had paused by his bench, even though she had a rather sulky round ticking creature with her who kept trying to drag her back to the cuckoo clocks.

'I'd be delighted,' said Silky. She turned the little handle and the lid of the box sprang open. A tiny wooden fairy wearing a gauzy white dress was standing on one leg. When the tinkly music started she began twirling round.

'She's lovely,' said Silky.

'Please, try another – and another!' said the elf, quite overcome.

Silky smiled and did so. All the music boxes had fairies, and they all danced to the same tune, but of course they were a little out of sync with each other. Silky gently touched each fairy on her small wooden head and the music immediately blended into one beautiful tune, and they pirouetted in perfect time with each other. Silky pointed at the fairies and they sprang from their boxes on to the workbench and danced together, twirling round in a circle and then leaping in the air simultaneously, their little wooden toes immaculately pointed.

'Oh, my!' said the elf. 'Oh, my, oh, my, oh, my! How did you make them do that?'

'I'm not really sure,' said Silky honestly. 'I think it's a Christmas Eve thing. It's very enjoyable.'

'Can we go and see the dolls and cuddly toys next?' Birdy asked hopefully.

There was a splendid selection of traditional dolls: exquisite china beauties with real hair and glass eyes and hand-sewn Victorian outfits; schoolgirl dolls with little leather satchels; bridesmaid dolls in pink and peach and sky-blue long dresses; princess dolls with little tiaras; bedtime dolls in cosy pyjamas and dressing gowns; and a whole nursery of baby dolls with soft tufty hair and gummy smiles. There were fairy dolls too, with wings and wands, though none were anywhere near as pretty as Silky.

'AWESOME!' said Birdy.

She wanted to linger over each and every one of the dolls, greeting them as if they were real little people. Moonface and Milo and Mia and Silky's clock grew rather bored because they weren't really into dolls.

'Come on, Birdy. I don't know what you see in dolls. They don't *do* anything,' said Milo, yawning.

'These ones do,' said Silky quietly. She pointed all around the doll room.

The china dolls tossed their long hair, blinked their glass eyes and said, 'How do you do?'

The schoolgirl dolls chanted together, 'One two is two, two twos are four, three twos are six.'

The bridesmaid dolls all clasped their posies and sang 'Here Comes the Bride' in tiny voices, while the princess dolls sang 'Let It Go' with great passion.

The bedtime dolls all yawned just like Milo and said, 'Time for bed!'

The babies all cried, 'Mama! Mama! Mama!'

The fairy dolls all flapped their wings and flew in the air, waving their wands.

Birdy whirled round, staring at them all, utterly enchanted. The elderly elves were delighted too.

'Is there any chance our dolls will retain these wondrous properties?' one elf asked hopefully.

'I'm afraid they will have lost their magic by the time children unwrap them on Christmas morning,' said Silky. 'However, *next* Christmas Eve I will try my hardest to remember each one, and then maybe the magic will stir within them again.'

'Oh, imagine what a lovely surprise that would be!' said Birdy.

Milo raised his eyebrows to Mia. 'I would find it pretty creepy if I were a little kid and my doll's eyes suddenly opened and it said, "How do you do?" to me in a prissy little voice!'

'Me too!' Mia giggled. 'Think of being fast asleep and then having your own lickle dolly belting out "Let It Go" for all she's worth!'

'Well, *I'd* think it was awesome!' said Birdy. 'And I bet most children would too!'

Milo and Mia didn't take such a scornful approach when they moved on to the cuddly toy section. They both still slept with teddies and had a soft spot for anything cute and snuggly. The elves in this room were putting the finishing touches to such a variety of species that the children stood still, marvelling.

There were giant teddy bears as big as they were and tiny teddy bears no larger than their thumbs. Some were cuddly with sweet smiles and soft limbs and big tummies. Some were astonishingly lifelike, with an upright stance and black snout and proper claws. If Pippin stood still, it would have been difficult to pick him out from all the toy bears. But of course Pippin couldn't possibly stand still. He capered round and round the bears delightedly, poking the cute ones in their tummies, but being more respectful to the really big bears just in case Silky brought them to life.

Pippin became super-excited when he spotted some plump, furry, brightly coloured bears – some red, some green, some purple, some blue!

'Oh, I had friends just like you when I was a baby cub in the Land of Bears!' Pippin said, trembling with excitement. 'But they were real live teddies and I could play with them.'

Everyone looked at Silky expectantly. She smiled and pointed at the colourful teddies. They suddenly leapt off the workbenches. Some were still half finished, with only one ear or without felt pads on their paws. They laughed and danced and threw their soft arms round Pippin and played a game of ring-a-ring-a-roses with him.

The children and Moonface and Silky and her clock wandered off to look at all the other animals. Birdy took a step backwards when she saw a very lifelike wolf with a big pink tongue hanging out between his sharp teeth.

'Please don't point your finger at him, Silky!' she said.

Silky clenched her fists to reassure her. Birdy particularly liked the fantasy animals, especially the fluffy unicorns in candyfloss pink.

Mia sniffed. 'They're nothing *like* unicorns,' she

said, but she gave each one a little stroke all the same. She was taken aback by the leopards and tigers and zebras, each perfectly spotted or striped, and the lion with a great mane was extraordinary.

'Could you make *them* come alive, Silky?' Mia begged.

'I'm not sure that would be a good idea,' said Silky.

'Duh!' said Milo. 'Even you wouldn't like to be savaged by a toy lion, Mia!'

There was a sudden cry from Birdy. Moonface rushed to her, ready to protect her from the jaws of a strange, shaggy creature with turquoise fur. But Birdy had cried out in utter joy, and the creature wasn't attacking her, he was licking her rapturously with his pink felt tongue.

Milo gasped, turning to Silky.

'Did you make him do that?' he asked.

'No, he did it all by himself,' she said. 'It's as if he recognised Birdy.'

'I know why!' said Mia. 'It's Gilbert, her dog!'

'That's not Gilbert!' said Milo. 'That dog's got much brighter fur and it's not all matted.'

'Birdy has a *turquoise* dog?' Moonface asked. 'What breed is it?'

'It's a toy, Moonface,' said Milo.

'A toy breed, like a chihuahua? But this dog's bigger than Birdy,' said Moonface.

'A toy,' Milo repeated. 'A toy that you play with. She had him for her second birthday and she's dragged him around with her ever since.'

The toy dog gave a series of happy woofs. They were slightly similar to bear cub grunts, but Pippin couldn't understand what he was saying. Yet Birdy could!

'He's not Gilbert – he's Albert!' said Birdy, giving him a hug.

'That's right,' said a smiley elf, nodding happily. His long white hair and beard had little turquoise streaks and he wore a bright turquoise elf suit. It was obviously his favourite colour. 'I specialise in making turquoise dogs for very special children. I remember making young Gilbert. He was such a happy little lad, though a bit mischievous at times. I tell all my dogs tales about their brothers and sisters and their special owners. Birdy is famous. Albert recognised her straight away. He wants to find an owner just like her.'

'Perhaps Albert could come and live with me and have Gilbert for his brother?' Birdy asked hopefully.

'I don't see how you could lug *two* dogs around. And if you took them both to bed, you'd get completely squashed,' said Mia.

'Then I'll have an extra-long play with him now!' said Birdy.

She stayed romping with Albert while everyone else went up to the construction department. It was testing time for all the tiny construction parts. Elves were sitting on the floor solemnly testing whether three toddler's plush bricks could stand steady in a tower. Others were making metal cranes and winding tiny handles to see if they could properly lift little crates. Some elves were slotting small plastic bricks together to make castles and cars and aeroplanes and spaceships, their hands moving so quickly they were just a blur. Each time one was completed they rang a little bell, and fresh elves rushed forward to deconstruct everything and put every single piece in the right packet.

Silky's clock liked the sound of the bell and started chiming too, so loudly that Silky had to pick it up and give it a gentle shake to make it stop. Then Albert came bouncing in, woofing excitedly, with Birdy running after him.

'Albert! Bad dog! Come back!' she shouted.

Albert seemed to think this command meant he should leap up and down on the huge construction tables and knock as many completed pieces over as he could. Little plastic bricks flew all over the place in a positive hailstorm. Even Silky's special magic power wasn't strong enough to quell him.

'Don't worry, everyone! I shall cast one of my magic spells!' said Moonface. 'Now, it should be easy-peasy. We learnt how to train a dog in reception class – it was everybody's favourite spell. Let me see . . .

'Wag your finger,
Wiggle your nose,
Dance a jig,
Then touch your . . . knees?'

'Toes!' everyone shouted.

They all tried the spell, doing all the actions, though they could hardly get the words out for laughing. It sounded as if Moonface had made the spell up on the spot (and perhaps he had), but Albert was so surprised to see everyone doing the oddest things that he stood still and stared and Birdy had the chance to grab his lead.

'You bad, bad, bad dog,' she said fondly, giving him a big cuddle.

'Perhaps we'd better take him back to the cuddly toy department,' said Silky.

'Oh, dear, I'd give anything to keep Albert!' said Birdy. 'But I suppose I have to let Santa give him to some other child.'

'You *have* got Gilbert, Birdy,' said Silky.

'I know,' said Birdy. 'But I wish I had both!'

Still, she went with Silky to return Albert and say goodbye to him. It took a very long time because she had to keep giving him an extra kiss and cuddle, but eventually they went to find the others, who were now in the electronic department.

The elves here were much younger and all dressed in black. They were all very pale, because they liked their job so much that they never went out anywhere.

'Oh, wow!' said Milo. 'Look, they've got *Dragonflame*! It's the amazing new game they're all talking about at school! If only Mum and Dad would let me have a game console!'

'Would you like to try it out?' the palest elf offered. 'It's super-cool!' His eyes shone behind his black-rimmed glasses.

'I'd absolutely love to!' said Milo.

'I'll play with you!' said Mia.

'I want to play too,' said Birdy.

'You're too little,' said Milo.

Mia and Milo settled down happily on a big black leather sofa, staring at a screen, their fingers poised on their handsets. Silky and Moonface looked baffled. Electronic games were unknown in the Enchanted Wood. They watched as two strange dragons flew towards each other. Moonface went up to the screen and put his hand on it.

'They're not real dragons,' he said, baffled. 'I don't understand.'

'I don't understand either,' said Silky. 'I think we're too little as well, Moonface.'

'I'm big!' said Pippin, standing as tall as he could. 'I want to play!'

'Well, come and play with me,' said Mia, but Pippin's paws were too slow and clumsy to work the handset.

'It's actually a silly game,' he said.

Silky's clock thought so too and ran around tick-tocking irritably. It found a door, slightly open. It stuck its foot in the crack and managed to open it up further. There was a strange whirring noise that puzzled it.

'Tick tock?' it said. It ran to investigate – and didn't come back.

'Clock? Where have you gone? Come here, silly!' Silky called.

She ran over to the door.

'Oh my goodness!' Silky exclaimed. 'Hey, everyone, you must come and look!'

CHAPTER
TWELVE

MILO AND Mia were too intent on their dragon fight
to be interested, but Birdy, Moonface and Pippin
all came scurrying. Silky's clock had discovered the
last toy department all by itself. Transport! And
the clock was being transported on an enormous
toy train down the entire length of the very long
room at breakneck speed. The train gave a whistle
and the clock chimed back – one, two, three, four,
five, six, seven, eight, nine, ten, eleven, twelve . . .
and then thirteen, fourteen, fifteen! It carried on
chiming while whizzing out of sight through a
tunnel and then chimed more as it came charging

back round the other side of the room. By the time the train slowed down and drew up beside Silky and Moonface and Pippin, the clock had almost lost its voice, and when it staggered off the train it had to lie flat on its back to recover.

'Was that fun, Clock?' Silky asked, stroking it.

Her clock kicked its legs weakly in the air and whispered, 'Tick tock!'

'Can we have a go?' Moonface asked the train. 'Come on, Pippin!'

They squatted on the train and it blew its whistle and chugged off.

'Whoopee!' Moonface shrieked. 'Faster, Train, faster!'

Silky shook her head at him fondly. Moonface was more like a little pixie toddler than a middle-aged gentleman, but what did it matter? She tucked her clock up in a skate bag to recover and wandered round the rest of the transport room, looking at the bikes and skateboards and roller skates, all demonstrated by obliging elves. She admired everything politely, though they didn't seem very exciting forms of transport to a fairy who could fly. But then she spotted a gleaming toy car just her size, a white Cadillac with pink upholstery. An elf opened the door for her and she climbed inside and switched the car on. It hummed expectantly. She clutched the steering wheel, put her foot on the pedal and then she was off!

Silky had heard about cars, though of course no one could drive one through the densely growing trees in the Enchanted Wood. She had even seen the odd car when she flew high above the treetops, but she had thought them rather odd and ugly noisy vehicles, and frighteningly huge. But this beautiful car simply hummed endearingly as she steered her way around the room.

She wasn't used to it, so at first she very nearly bumped into counters and almost collided with an elf testing an electric scooter, but after several minutes she got the hang of it and drove round confidently, even having a go at racing the train. It blew its whistle at her, and Silky found the car's horn and honked back at it.

'Do you want a ride, Pippin?' she called, but he was experimenting with roller skates now.

'What about you, Moonface?' Silky asked, but he was climbing back on the train.

'Birdy, you'll come, won't you?' Silky called.

Birdy was busy trying to ride a proper bike. She was a demon on her trike, but Mia and Milo never let her have a go on their own proper bicycles in case she crashed into something and buckled the front wheels. But here Birdy had an obliging elf on either side to stop her wobbling and was concentrating on mastering real cycling.

'Then perhaps you would like to join me, sir?' Silky said to the elf who had opened the door for her.

The elf was quite overcome. He had test driven thousands of cars in his time and had patiently demonstrated them to many potential customers. He still trembled with pride and joy remembering the time the great Santa himself had squeezed into the car and driven a few metres, ho-ho-hoing all the time. But the elf had rarely been invited to be a passenger in one of his cars, and never by anyone as beautiful and gracious as this lovely fairy.

'It would give me immense pleasure, madam,' he said, and climbed in beside her, almost overcome.

By the time they'd raced round the whole room several times, they were both shouting for sheer joy at the speed of the car, calling each other Hot Wheels and Fairy Queen as if they'd been friends for years.

When Milo and Mia came looking for them at last, Birdy had managed to pedal all by herself for a few seconds, Pippin was zigzagging crazily around yelling, 'Look at me!' and Moonface was actually taking a turn at driving the train himself, his white face flushed almost scarlet.

Milo and Mia joined him on the train for one circuit, and then Milo tried out an electric bike even though he knew he was officially too young to ride it. Mia brushed up her skateboarding skills, managing to jump up and twirl round and land back on the board again, a trick she'd never managed before.

She was having a wonderful time, but she was still eager to get to the reindeer to see them being fed.

'Exactly what time do the reindeer have their feed?' Mia asked the skateboard elf.

He shrugged. 'When they're hungry?' he suggested.

Obviously time didn't really exist here, like in the Enchanted Wood, but Mia was sure they'd been wandering around the various departments for quite a while.

'Shall we go and see the reindeer now?' she called out to everyone.

She had to call several times, but at last Moonface climbed off the train, Milo dismounted from his bike and Silky gave her Hot Wheels a grateful kiss on the cheek, stepped daintily out of the car and unbuckled Pippin's roller skates for him.

'Now, I'll wake up my clock,' Silky said, looking round. 'I tucked him up in one of the navy skate bags.'

'Which ones?' said Milo.

'They were . . . over there!' said Silky, her voice suddenly high-pitched. She pointed to where the pile of skate bags had been. But there were no navy ones there. No green or red ones either. There wasn't a single skate bag left in the whole room.

Silky clutched Hot Wheels. 'There was a whole pile of skate bags there!' she gasped. 'Please can you tell me where they are *now?*'

'They'll have been taken to be wrapped and then labelled, ready for dispatch,' he said.

'But my little clock was fast asleep in one of them!' said Silky, and she lost all her usual composure and started crying.

'Don't worry, Silky! Surely all you have to do is point to where the bag was and magic him back?' said Milo.

'I don't think my magic's as powerful as that!' Silky wept, though she tried and tried, pointing desperately in thin air.

'Moonface, can't you make one of your magic spells?' Mia asked.

'I don't know any spells to conjure up a clock in a skate bag!' said Moonface. 'I'm sure we were never taught that at Enchanter School.'

'Then let's run to see if he's being wrapped!' said Birdy.

So they gabbled thank yous to the helpful toy-department elves and rushed to the right-hand side of the building. They tried the wrapping department first. It was huge, on several floors, and all the elves there were working at double-quick time, wrapping every gift and labelling it. There were small elves in training, wrapping pocket-sized presents, presided over by a kindly elf woman who showed them how to fold the wrap neatly and tie ribbons. One of the littlest elves had managed to tie

his own hands up with sticky tape and she was gently unpeeling it, shaking her head at him.

Most of the elves were middle-sized and so experienced that they could chat away as they wrapped, often singing along to the Christmas music playing all the time. 'We Wish You a Merry Christmas' seemed a particular favourite, but Birdy didn't join in, too worried about Silky's clock to sing.

The tallest elves worked together on tricky gifts like rocking horses and toy cars. They were laughing and joking about what they were going to do for their week's holiday – they didn't have to go back to work until the New Year.

Sweetmeat was darting between all the sections, checking labels and making sure each gift was securely wrapped. Silky ran to him and explained that her clock had been taken away by mistake. Sweetmeat did his best to calm her, took a megaphone and bellowed a message to all the elves.

'SUDDEN EMERGENCY! A SMALL TICKING CLOCK HAS BEEN MISTAKEN

FOR A GIFT. HAS ANYONE RECENTLY WRAPPED ONE? IT MIGHT STILL BE TUCKED IN A SKATE BAG, SO WOULD ALL ELVES DEALING WITH TRANSPORT KINDLY CHECK ALL BAGS?'

The elves all obligingly checked, not grumbling at all even though it meant they'd have to do some serious rewrapping, but shook their heads.

Silky called out to her clock in case he was fast asleep inside the skate bag.

'CLOCK! DEAR CLOCK! PLEASE WAKE UP AND CHIME AS LOUD AS YOU CAN SO I CAN FIND YOU!' she shouted.

Everyone else shouted to the clock too, and then Sweetmeat raised his hand and cupped his ear so that everyone stopped looking and listened. Even the Christmas music stopped. There was silence, with not even the tiniest tick tock.

'What shall I do if it's lost for ever?' Silky wept. 'My own dear clock. I've had it ever since my wings first started sprouting! Its steady little ticks lull me to sleep every night! What shall I do without it?'

'Don't despair, madam fairy! It will have progressed to the despatch department. We will find it there,' Sweetmeat assured her.

'But what if it's *been* despatched already?' Silky sobbed.

'Impossible,' Sweetmeat said firmly. 'I am positive not a single child has requested a skate bag containing a small clock. It won't have a label and therefore cannot be despatched.'

'There now, Silky! Listen to this fine fellow! We will find your funny old clock, just you wait and see,' said Moonface, offering her his white handkerchief. He tenderly wiped her damp face and then took her arm.

They all trooped after Sweetmeat. Birdy clutched Mia's hand. She was nearly in tears herself.

'We will find it, won't we?' she asked Mia. 'Silky's so upset!'

'Don't worry – I'm sure her clock will be in this despatch place, chiming its head off,' said Mia. She wasn't totally sure of it, but she wanted to comfort poor Birdy. Her own stomach was in a knot of anxiety. They were all really worried. Even Pippin was drooping.

The despatch department was the biggest in the whole complex. They peered down at it from a balcony. There was a gigantic wavy outline painted across the entire floor, marked into sections. It seemed vaguely familiar to Milo. It was like a huge map. Then he realised it was exactly that – a map of the whole of Great Britain – and an army of elves were dashing about, loading huge piles of shiny parcels here and there. Sometimes they were too eager, and the parcel towers swayed and collapsed, tumbling everywhere. The elves scurried to rebuild them, shaking each parcel warily in case anything had got broken.

If there was any doubt, a senior elf would shout, 'Replacement needed – another doll's china tea set for Charlotte in East Sussex! Quickly now!' or, 'Replacement required – new musical bell for baby Phoebe in Warwickshire!' An especially speedy elf would dash to the right toy department, find another tea set or bell, rush it to wrapping and then charge back with it in double-quick time.

Then further elves would start loading presents on to big trolleys, marked 'Journey One', 'Journey Two', 'Journey Three' – many, many, many journeys.

'How on earth can Santa make all those journeys in just one night?' said Milo.

'The reindeer will be exhausted,' said Mia.

'Do you think he'll have time to come to us?' Birdy asked anxiously.

'I expect you'll be visited on Journey One, because you're staying so close to the Enchanted Wood,' said Moonface comfortingly. He gave Pippin a little hug. 'Here's hoping he hovers halfway down the Magic Faraway Tree and delivers our presents too!'

Silky was still so distraught that she wasn't paying attention. She was calling mournfully, 'Clock! It's me, Silky! Oh, please call out to me, my dear clock!'

Sweetmeat commandeered a trolley, and the obliging elves pushed him around the entire complex while he called out on his megaphone. He bellowed his message about the missing clock again and again. He found a special despatch of skate bags going to a football academy and personally shook each one, but none had a ticking clock tumbling about inside.

'Oh, Clock, are you lost for ever?' Silky sobbed, when the entire despatch room had been searched.

'Don't despair, dear madam fairy! There is one more possibility!' said Sweetmeat. 'Come with me.'

He steered her right to the end of the despatch department, the others following. There was a sign marked 'To the Stables'. Mia quivered. But there was also a door with another notice: 'Lost Property'.

Sweetmeat opened this door with a flourish and they all peered inside. It was a surprisingly small room, not much bigger than a cupboard, with scarcely any parcels on the three shelves. Most of them looked rather dusty, as if they'd been there for years. An extremely elderly elf was in a rocking chair behind the counter, eyes closed, snoring gently.

'Is this *it*?' said Milo. 'But it's got hardly any lost property!'

'Exactly,' said Sweetmeat. 'I pride myself on the efficiency of our wonderful elfin workforce. But just occasionally there is a little blip in our system. I like to feel I am prepared for every possibility. We will find the clock!'

'But it's not here!' said Silky, peering at the parcels on the shelves. Some were too small; some were too big. None had the big triangular shape of a skate bag or the small round shape of a clock.

'Oh, Clock, Clock, Clock!' Silky cried aloud.

There was a sudden stirring and scuffling behind the counter – and then the tremendously loud shriek of an alarm going off. The snoring elf woke up in a fright and grabbed something behind the counter, at his feet.

'It's the new parcel! Duck, everyone! I think it's going to explode!' he gasped.

But Silky leapt right over the counter with one flutter of her wings and grabbed a tightly wrapped parcel that was making an ear-splitting noise. She ripped it, opened the zip of the bag and brought out her poor clock, with it still screaming. She touched its little button nose and the terrible noise stopped – to be replaced by joyful chiming as it realised it was in Silky's arms.

'Oh, Clock, Clock, Clock!' Silky crooned.

It tried to chime and tick and tock all at the same time.

'Calm down, Clock dear, or you'll bust your springs,' said Silky. 'I am so, so sorry I left you in that skate bag. It was very silly of me. I swear it will never happen again. Please say you forgive me?'

Silky's clock was so eager to reassure her that he got the hiccups. 'Tick tock, tick tock, tick tock, tick tick tick tock!' it said, and then covered its mouth in embarrassment as the children giggled.

'I knew we would find you, Mr Clock!' said Sweetmeat, swelling with pride.

'Thank you so, so much, dear Sweetmeat!' said Silky, and she kissed his cheek.

Sweetmeat went very pink, a silly smile on his face.

'Any time, dear madam fairy,' he said, sweeping her a bow.

'Can we go and see the reindeer now?' Mia asked.

'In just a minute, Mia,' said Silky. She thanked the sleepy old elf behind the counter, who explained that he'd been keeping an eye on the new parcel, pondering which shelf to put it on. He seemed a little sad that it had now been claimed, as he had so few parcels to look after, but he cheered up when Sweetmeat said he could keep the skate bag if it wasn't wanted elsewhere.

Moonface insisted on shaking both elves' hands, and Pippin tested out each shelf in Lost Property, pretending they were little bear caves.

'Can I just nip back to the electronics department and carry on playing *Dragonflame* for a bit?' Milo asked.

'And I'd like to go back to the cuddly toys and see if I can train Albert to sit if I offer him a treat,' said Birdy, who still had a few gingerbread crumbs down her front.

'But we've seen them already. We haven't seen the reindeer yet!' said Mia. 'I really want to see them being fed.'

'And so you shall,' said Sweetmeat. 'We'd best be quick. They will be doing their practice flight soon. Come with me, little miss.'

Mia followed him eagerly down the passageway to the reindeer stables. She smelt a lovely warm smell of animals and hay. There they were, big, fine brown reindeer, each with an impressive spread of antlers. Mia stood still, wanting them to have time to look at her and see she was a friend.

'Don't be afraid – they won't hurt you,' said Sweetmeat, misunderstanding.

'I know,' Mia said softly. 'Oh, they're so beautiful.'

They were all munching their meal enthusiastically, a big mound of moss and lichen. Every third or fourth mouthful, they drank from a large bowl of water with a golden sheen.

'What is it they're drinking?' Mia asked.

'Ah! That's Santa's special strengthening cordial, made to his own secret recipe. They're flying at full speed from nightfall tonight to dawn tomorrow, with very little time for resting. The cordial gives them stamina,' Sweetmeat explained. 'Doesn't it, fine fellow?' he added, gently scratching between the antlers of the reindeer nearest him.

The reindeer moved his head happily, enjoying the scratch.

'Do you think he'd let me do that?' Mia said hopefully.

'I'm sure he would,' said Sweetmeat.

Mia had to climb a little set of steps to reach, and then scratched him, thrilling at the feel of the reindeer's soft velvety head. He blew out of his nostrils, showing he was pleased, and then put his head back in his food bowl. The reindeer were all eating calmly enough, but Mia saw they had a tenseness about them, and several were pawing the ground.

'They know what they're going to be doing, don't they?' she said to Sweetmeat.

'Yes, they're very excited. It's a great honour to be chosen as the Christmas reindeer. These are a new strong pack from the Land of—'

'The Frozen North!' Mia said, finishing his sentence. 'We saw them there! I so hoped they were the same ones.'

'They are especially fit and sturdy. Santa is very pleased. There are more presents than ever to deliver and it's always a big challenge reaching everyone, but these reindeer will serve him well,' said Sweetmeat.

'So what happens after Christmas?' Mia asked. 'Do they fly somewhere else?'

'We leave it up to them. Some fly back to their homes. Others seek out new pastures. And some stay here with us. We have many forests and fields where they can roam freely and breed. We love seeing the calves in the spring.'

'Do baby reindeer have antlers?' Mia asked. She had once seen a cow giving birth and she thought antlers might make the process tricky.

'I don't think they start to grow until they're about two years old,' said Sweetmeat. 'My children love to play with the calves when they're old enough.'

'Oh, the lucky things!' said Mia. 'I think reindeer are my new favourite animal. Who couldn't love them?'

Then she remembered another animal that lived in the Land of the Frozen North.

'You don't get any wolves in the Land of Toys, do you?' Mia asked. 'Real ones?'

Sweetmeat shook his head firmly.

'Anyway, you could simply fly away if any fierce wolves came prowling, couldn't you?' Mia murmured to the reindeer she was stroking.

The reindeer nodded as if he could understand every word. Mia ran her hands over his strong brown back.

'I wonder how you do it?' she said. 'My friend Silky can fly, but she's got wings. Do you have wings too and they just sprout when you leap in the air?'

The reindeer blew down his nose, finding this funny. Mia could feel the muscles in his back and see the strength in his restless legs.

'I suppose it's just like a super power?' Mia said thoughtfully.

'I think you must have a super power too, Miss Mia,' said Sweetmeat. 'You have such a knack of talking to animals and making them respond. Wild reindeer can be unpredictable. Many of my elves are a little scared of them, but you are fearless.'

Mia felt her heart thumping with pride. When Birdy and Pippin and Moonface and Silky (carrying her clock) came into the stables she loved showing them how to be quiet and wait patiently until the reindeer had sized them up and got used to them. Pippin had to be extra patient because the reindeer were very suspicious of bears, even very small ones, and shifted restlessly from hoof to hoof, but Mia managed to calm them all. Pippin was quiet too, and hid behind Mia, worried about all those huge antlers waving above him.

Milo had been gone for so long that Moonface had to go and fetch him. He came back rather bleary-eyed, but very happy.

'*Dragonflame* is the best game *ever*!' he said.

'How could you prefer playing a game to being with a live animal?' Mia said.

'I've just had a lovely game being with a *toy* animal, but he came alive for me!' said Birdy. 'I know it's mean of me, and some other child will be hoping for a wonderful puppy like Albert for Christmas, but I *wish* he could be Gilbert's little brother and live with us!'

'What do you want for Christmas, Pippin?' Mia asked. 'I bet it's the biggest pot of honey in the world!'

Pippin licked his lips at the thought, but for once Mia was wrong.

'I'd like a cuddly teddy and we'd snuggle up together at night and play games all day long,' said Pippin.

'What about you, Moonface? What would you like?' Milo asked.

'I'd like my own train!' Moonface said, smiling at the memory of all those rides.

'And what would you like, Silky?' Birdy asked.

'I just want my own clock to be safe and sound,' said Silky, clutching it fondly. The clock replied with a sleepy, 'Tick tock, tick tock,' tired out by all its adventures.

Then they all heard heavy footsteps behind

them – the sort of footsteps that a pair of big black boots might make. They turned and saw a large gentleman with twinkling blue eyes and a long white beard, dressed in a dashing red robe edged in white. Santa Claus! Not an image on a screen – the real live Santa himself.

They all gasped in awe. The clock even missed a tick and a tock.

'This is the father of Christmas himself – our dear Santa Claus,' Sweetmeat announced unnecessarily.

Santa smiled at them all cheerily. 'Hello, my dears. Have you enjoyed your little tour of the Land of Toys?'

They murmured gratefully, feeling very shy.

'Have you seen anything you'd particularly like to be given tomorrow?' Santa asked, inclining his head, ready to listen.

They all had, but somehow it seemed impolite and greedy to make demands.

'What about you, little Birdy?' said Santa.

Birdy was so thrilled that he really did know her name.

'Anything at all,' she said. She didn't quite know what to call him face to face. 'Don't worry about it, Sir Santa Christmas. But perhaps it should be very little, because our holiday cottage hasn't got a very big chimney.'

'Don't you worry about it, my dear. I know I'm quite a tubby gentleman.' Santa patted his big tummy. 'So many mince pies are left out for me! I've got such a sweet tooth that I can't resist them. But I promise I'm a dab hand at getting down the narrowest chimneys. I just s-q-u-e-e-z-e myself small enough.' Santa demonstrated, taking a tremendous deep breath . . . and right before their eyes he shrank himself smaller than Birdy, skinnier than Silky. He stayed like that for a moment or two while they gawped at him, and then breathed out and grew right back to his proper cuddly size.

'Does the Christmas present shrink too?' Milo asked.

'Yes, it does, just until I put it under the Christmas tree,' said Santa.

'But what about places that don't have chimneys?' Pippin asked, thinking about his little bear cave in the Magic Faraway Tree.

'I can squeeze through windows or even creep under doors if necessary,' said Santa.

'I wonder if you'd be willing to share your magic spell, sir?' Moonface asked humbly. 'We never learnt anything like that when I was at Enchanter School.'

'I'm afraid it's simply willpower,' said Santa. 'I'm so determined to reach every child that I somehow make it happen.'

Moonface took a deep breath and tried to make himself smaller. He held his breath until he glowed red in the face, but he didn't shrink by so much as a millimetre.

'Oh, dear,' he said, hanging his head. 'I'm a bit rubbish at magic, aren't I?'

'Never mind, Moonface. You still make the best Toffee Shocks in the whole world,' Silky comforted him. 'Have you got a little bag of them in your pocket by any chance? If Santa has a sweet tooth, I'm sure he'd love one.'

'Aha!' said Moonface, producing a bag of Toffee Shocks and offering it to Santa, then to Sweetmeat, then to everyone else – even Silky's clock.

There was a pause in the conversation as everyone chewed intently. Then the delicious sweets started exploding in everybody's mouths, and Sweetmeat jumped in the air and Santa shook with laughter.

'Ho, ho, ho!' he spluttered. 'What do you mean, you're rubbish at magic! That's fantastic! You must give me the recipe!'

'Certainly!' said Moonface, though he'd never told anyone before how he made his Toffee Shocks, not even Silky.

He whispered the recipe in Santa's ear and they shook hands.

'Now I'm afraid I must go on a test run with my special reindeer,' Santa said. He stood up straight, did a few stretches and then ran on the spot, surprisingly light in spite of his heavy boots. Then he clapped his hands and the reindeer stopped grazing and stood to attention. He led them out of the long tunnel to where a magnificent, huge sleigh was waiting. It was laden with cardboard boxes.

'Are they presents?' Milo asked, puzzled, because they weren't wrapped at all.

'No, no, they're just old packing boxes,' Sweetmeat explained. 'It's just a trial run, to get the reindeer used to pulling the sleigh. Until they get the feel of racing in unison, they might make the sleigh tip so that the boxes start tumbling out. We wouldn't want to lose any real presents.'

Mia was going from one reindeer to another,

scratching their heads and wishing them luck.

'What happens to them when you go down the chimneys, Santa? Do they just kind of hover above the roof?' she asked.

'Mostly, yes. But if there's a big, strong, flat roof, we'll land on it and they can have a little rest and I'll give them a carrot or two,' said Santa. 'Don't worry about them, my dear. They'll be fine.'

'And will you be fine too, Santa?' said Birdy. 'You look about as old as my grandad and I know he couldn't stay up all night delivering presents. He gets puffed when he just walks down the road.'

'Bless you, sweetheart! I've been going strong for hundreds of years – and I daresay I've still got hundreds of years ahead of me,' said Santa. 'Now farewell, everyone. And happy Christmas!'

'Happy Christmas!' everyone chorused.

Santa leapt into his sleigh and took the reins. He shook them lightly.

'Off we go, reindeer!' he shouted.

They broke into a run, tentative at first, but when they got into step they suddenly galloped, faster and faster, until they shot into the air, the sleigh lifting too, up and up and up. They were so high now that they could hardly be seen. Santa's robe was just a little red spot, but they heard his 'Ho, ho, ho!' echoing down to the ground.

Everyone waved and wished him luck. When they went back inside the huge toy factory they saw the elves scurrying around the giant map of Britain, piling brightly wrapped packages as fast as they could. A couple of younger elves were a little careless and one of the piles wavered and then tumbled down.

'No, no, no!' said Sweetmeat. 'Excuse me, everyone! I have to show them how to do it properly! Goodbye! I hope you've enjoyed your tour.'

'We've had the most marvellous time. Thank you very much,' said Silky, on behalf of everyone. She smiled at them. 'All the elves are so busy now. I think we'd better go home and leave them to it.'

'Perhaps we could have just one more trip on the train?' Moonface suggested.

'Perhaps not,' said Silky. 'We've got to wrap our own presents, Moonface, and put up all our decorations. And I'm going to make my own fairy Christmas pudding. I'll let you stir it if you like.'

'Can I stir it too?' Pippin asked.

'Of course you can,' said Silky.

'We're going to be making our own Christmas pudding too,' said Milo. 'But not that dark, fruity sort. Ours is going to be banoffee pie, yum, yum.'

'I hope Mum hasn't got up early and started making it by herself,' said Mia, and then clapped her hand over her mouth. 'Hey, we've been gone *ages*!

Mum and Dad must have got up by now.'

'It's OK – you know time stops when we're in the Enchanted Wood,' said Milo.

Silky's clock started chiming indignantly to show them that *it* hadn't stopped.

'Let's get back as quick as quick, just to make sure!' said Mia.

They rushed to the entrance and found the top of the ladder back to the Magic Faraway Tree. They clambered down as fast as they could, shivering now in the sudden cold. They slid down Moonface's slippery-slip as a shortcut and then hurtled out on to the snow. It was still dark and they stood still for a moment, not sure which way to go.

'Follow me,' said Silky. 'Moonface, Pippin, Clock, you start getting out all my mixing bowls and spoons while I see the children safely home.'

She flew above them like their own little guiding star. In no time they were back in the lane and then in just a few steps they'd arrived in the cottage's back garden. They could just make out the shapes of their snow angels and Milo's snowman and their own footsteps crossing this way and that.

'Don't worry!' Silky whispered. 'Happy Christmas!'

She waited until they were all on the doorstep and then waved her arms in the air. The snow rose slightly and then settled itself. There was no trace of the snow angels and snowman. The snow lay thick and even and untouched.

The children waved thankfully at Silky and then crept indoors and up the stairs. They could hear Dad snoring gently and Mum murmuring in her sleep. It was still the very start of Christmas Eve.

CHAPTER THIRTEEN

THE FAMILY went out to the nearest town straight after breakfast to buy a turkey before they all sold out.

'Sorry you can't have your little run outside,' said Mum.

'Oh, that's OK, Mum,' said Milo, slightly uncomfortably.

'We can't really run in the snow anyway,' said Mia.

'And we're a bit tired,' said Birdy, giving an enormous yawn.

They got rather bored trailing around the hot, crowded supermarket, but when the Christmas food was safely in the boot of the car Dad drove them out to a garden centre so they could choose a little Christmas tree for the cottage – and all the decorations.

'We must have a proper fairy on top of the tree,' said Birdy. She was happy when they found a little doll with long hair and tiny wings and a silver dress. 'Though she's not nearly as pretty as Silky,' Birdy whispered to Mia.

The children were allowed to decorate the tree themselves and then they helped make the banoffee pie for tomorrow.

'Can we make mince pies too?' Birdy begged.

'I didn't think you liked them,' said Mum.

'No, I don't – but Santa does!' said Birdy.

'Well, I'm sure lots of other children will leave him a mince pie on a plate tonight,' said Dad. 'He's probably heartily sick of mince pies now.'

'No, he still loves them, even though he says they make him tubby,' said Birdy, giggling.

'You and your imagination!' said Dad.

He was in such a good mood though that he

offered to go down to the little general shop in the nearby village and buy a jar of mincemeat all the same.

'And while you're there, Dad, could you see if they've got any carrots?' Mia asked.

'But we've got parsnips and Brussels sprouts and cauliflower and peas. We don't need another veg,' said Mum.

'She wants it for Santa's reindeer,' said Birdy. 'Lots of carrots, because there are eight of them.'

'Nine,' said Milo.

'Don't start that again,' said Dad. He started singing 'Rudolph the Red-Nosed Reindeer'.

Birdy tried counting on her fingers as Dad said the reindeer names.

'There, eight!' she said.

'Nine,' Milo insisted. 'Because Rudolph's the main reindeer, see? I'm right, aren't I, Dad?'

'That's just in the song. Actually there are twelve real reindeer. I counted them carefully in the stables,' Mia whispered.

She wasn't very good at whispering and Dad heard.

'You kids and your imaginary games!' he said – but he brought back a jar of mincemeat and a huge bunch of carrots from the shop even so.

They baked the mince pies, ate toasted sandwiches for lunch then went out for a snowy walk – Mum and Dad and the three children. They walked the opposite way from the Enchanted Wood, over several fields.

'Shall we build a snow scarecrow?' said Dad.

'We *could* do,' said Milo. He was remembering the tale of the boy who went up the ladder at the top of the Magic Faraway Tree and got captured by a snowman. 'No, let's have a snow fight instead.'

They had a little friendly snowball battle, Mum and Dad against Milo, Mia and Birdy. The sun came out, so it wasn't too bitterly cold, though the snow stayed firm.

'It's great sledging weather,' said Dad, sighing. 'If I had enough wood, I'd make you a makeshift sledge, kids.'

'Well, there wouldn't be much point – there aren't any hills around here,' Mum said. 'The fields are quite flat, and obviously you can't sledge in the Enchanted Wood.' Mum paused. 'I wonder why it's called that?'

'Maybe it's full of fairies and elves and pixies, eh, Birdy?' said Dad, picking her up and twirling her round.

'It is, Dad, it is!' said Birdy, wondering if he'd somehow found out about the Magic Faraway Tree and all their special friends.

Milo and Mia knew Dad was simply teasing.

'Ha, ha, Dad. I expect there are lickle fairies flitting around all over the place,' said Milo.

'Ooh, perhaps we'll be able to make a wish!' said Mia, in a funny baby voice.

'Stop being silly!' Birdy hissed. 'You know it's our magic place.'

'Of course it's magic, Birdy,' said Dad.

'What's it like, really?' said Mum.

'Oh, it's just a perfectly ordinary wood,' said Dad, because it had seemed exactly that to him. He saw Birdy looking puzzled. 'But *maybe* there were fairies hiding, peeping out at me all the time,' he added.

'Maybe there were,' said Birdy. 'I just happen to *know* a fairy and she's the loveliest person ever, and that's true, true, true!'

Milo and Mia held their breath. Mum and Dad were looking at her strangely. Birdy burst out laughing at all their faces.

'It's the fairy on our Christmas tree!' she said, and laughed so much she fell over in the snow and rolled around, kicking her legs. She was so happy that she'd made a joke and they'd all been taken in by it.

Milo and Mia started rolling around in the snow and laughing too.

'Get up, you silly sausages – you're getting soaking wet!' said Dad.

They went back to the warm cottage and then played some of the old board games that were stacked in a cupboard. They particularly liked Snakes and Ladders, although Birdy squealed whenever she landed on a snake.

'Imagine going up the ladder in the Faraway Tree and finding the Land of Snakes!' she whispered to Milo and Mia, shuddering.

'Horrible, slippery, slimy snakes!' said Milo, pretending his arm was a snake and winding it round Birdy. He flickered his finger at Birdy like a tongue. She squealed even louder.

'Snakes are not the slightest bit slimy,' said Mia impatiently. 'They might be cold-blooded, but they feel quite warm and dry.'

'Stop it now, Milo! You'll give Birdy nightmares,' said Mum.

'We're not going to dream about silly old snakes tonight. We're going to dream about Santa Claus,' said Dad. He stuck out his tummy and strode round the room comically. 'Ho, ho, ho! Have you all been good, children? Shall I leave you a present? Not if you've been naughty!'

'Oh, Dad! Santa's not a bit like that!' said Birdy.

They left Santa *two* mince pies that night, plus a cheese and pickle sandwich in case he fancied anything savoury, with a can of cola to slake Santa's thirst. Mia went to the trouble of scrubbing the carrots and laid them out in a big dish, with a few Brussels sprouts as garnish.

'We're giving Santa and his reindeer a royal feast this year!' said Mum. 'Still, I suppose it's hungry work delivering all those presents.'

The children hung up their Christmas stockings on the end of their beds. They were the decorative felt kind, bigger than an actual woolly sock, but not enormous.

'They don't really hold much, do they?' said Milo. 'What if Santa decides to give us something quite big?'

'He'll leave any big presents under the Christmas tree,' said Mum.

'Always supposing you're getting any,' said Dad, but it was clear he was just teasing.

The children were allowed to stay up later than usual, and then when they went to bed Mum and Dad took turns reading them Christmassy stories. When they were eventually tucked up in bed they waited for a while, and then all crowded into Birdy's attic room and peered out of her window, looking up at the sky, hoping for a glimpse of Santa Claus and his reindeer.

After a long while they saw a little glowing light in the distance, and a flash of red. But it wasn't Santa, it was Silky in a red cloak, come to say goodnight. She smiled when she saw all three children with their noses pressed against the window and she blew them all kisses.

'*Happy Christmas!*' she mouthed to each of them, and then she waved and flew away again – upwards! They stared as Silky rose higher and higher, above the treetops.

'I think she's going to meet Santa!' said Milo.

'Oh, if only we could go too!' said Mia.

'Lucky, lucky Silky!' said Birdy. 'Do you think I could be a fairy when I grow up?'

Milo and Mia would normally have laughed at her, but it was Christmas Eve, and they were feeling fond of their little sister.

'Maybe, if you try really hard,' said Mia. 'And I'm going to be the greatest animal naturalist in the whole world.'

'And I'm going to be the fastest runner in the world – at sprints, and middle and long distance,' said Milo.

They had a big hug and then they all went to bed. They planned to wake up very early in the morning again, to check that Santa had really come in the night and left them presents, and then they were going to creep out of the house and go to visit all their Magic Faraway Tree friends to wish them a happy Christmas and give them their chocolate presents. Milo had them ready in a brown paper bag. Mia had drawn some holly and stars all over it with her felt tips to make it look more festive.

Milo set the alarm on his watch for 6 o'clock, though he was certain he'd wake up very early anyway. He stirred when the alarm rang and managed to switch it off – but went back to sleep immediately. Mia and Birdy didn't wake up either. They had all been up so early on Christmas Eve and had had such a busy time that they were exhausted. Mum and Dad had to wake them up gently much later.

'My goodness, fancy sleeping in on Christmas Day! Grab your stockings and duvets and come into our bed so we can see you opening your presents!' they called.

Milo, Mia and Birdy sat up sleepily and reached for their stockings. They were bulky with presents! They were suddenly wide awake and went rushing into the big bedroom. Mum and Dad sat up at the pillow end, sipping their morning tea, while the children huddled at the other end of the bed, their duvets wrapped round them for warmth.

They delved into their stockings, shouting and laughing. Milo got a stopwatch, a huge bar of chocolate, a toy iguanodon for his dinosaur collection, a ball, a pack of cards and a funny adventure story. He was especially thrilled with the stopwatch because he could time his running.

Mia got a proper wristwatch, a big bag of chocolate Brazil nuts, a toy horse, a drawing pad and felt tip pens, and a book about cats. She was really glad she had her own watch now and wouldn't have to keep asking Milo what the time was – and very pleased about the cat book.

Birdie got a blue bead bracelet, three small packets of sweets, a family of toy rabbits, a pink pencil with a fluffy feather and a picture book about a tiger who

A CHRISTMAS ADVENTURE

came to tea. She couldn't decide which present was her favourite because she liked them all so much.

The children gave Mum and Dad their presents, feeling a bit bashful because they did look very homemade, but Mum and Dad seemed absolutely thrilled with their purse and wallet and bookmarks and pictures and said they were their best presents ever.

Then they all had a cuddle together at the proper end of the bed. Mia slipped out first and ran downstairs to see if the carrots were still on the plate. They were all gone, the Brussels sprouts too. There were just a few crumbs left of the mince pies, and the can of cola was empty. She grinned happily. Then she saw more presents under the Christmas tree. There was a big boxy present with a label saying, 'To Milo with love from Santa'. There were *five* presents labelled, 'To Birdy with love from Santa'. But there was just a very small square flat present saying, 'To Mia with love from Santa'. She felt it. The present seemed to be just thick paper. It was probably just a Christmas card.

Mia couldn't help feeling horribly disappointed. Didn't Santa like her as much as Milo and Birdie? She had to screw her face up to stop herself bursting into tears. She told herself firmly that she was being silly. She'd already had lovely presents in her stocking. Santa had certainly *seemed* to like her. He probably just couldn't make up his mind what to give her. She knew she couldn't *really* have a puppy because Mum and Dad went out to work – and as if she could ever have her own pony! Santa had probably given her a gift token so she could choose anything else she wanted.

Mia tried to comfort herself, but she still felt as if she had stones in her stomach. She wanted to rush to Mum and have a good cry – but she felt she was too old to make such a fuss, and she'd be spoiling Christmas for everyone else.

'This is going to be a *happy* Christmas!' she said determinedly, and she took a deep breath and ran back upstairs.

'Santa gave the reindeer all the carrots!' Mia announced. 'And he's left us presents under the tree!'

'Ooh, let's get them!' said Milo.

The stones banged together in Mia's tummy. She couldn't face opening her card just yet, not in front of everyone.

'Why don't we wait till after breakfast?' she said.

'Good idea, Mia!' said Dad. 'Come on, you lot, up you get. I'll get cracking on the bacon sandwiches.'

Both Milo and Birdy had a peep at their presents first. Milo couldn't help hoping his really was a game console at long last. He wanted it so much he was a little scared of opening it, just in case he was wrong. Birdy was a bit worried about her five presents as well, though the biggest one felt very promising. She hoped she was right. She took Gilbert to have a sniff at the parcel and he looked pleased. But what if she was wrong? And she wasn't too sure about the other presents. There were three little ones, and a medium one too – all quite squashy. Perhaps they were clothes. She hoped they weren't itchy woollen socks with a jumper to match, like the ones Granny knitted her last year.

They all relaxed a little over their bacon

sandwiches. They always had them for Christmas breakfast because they were quick and easy, meaning Mum and Dad could concentrate on preparing the turkey and all the vegetables for Christmas dinner.

'Right, present time!' said Dad.

'Aren't you going to have your second cup of coffee?' said Mia.

'We'll have our coffee while you open your presents,' said Dad.

The children looked at him anxiously. Milo and Birdy were still keen to open their presents even if Mia was dreading it, but they were also very much wanting to slip off to the Enchanted Wood to wish all their friends a merry Christmas and give them their presents. They were also very curious to see which magic land was at the top of the tree. It had to be somewhere special on Christmas Day!

'Could we just have one little run in the lane first?' Milo said quickly.

'But it's still snowy outside,' said Mum.

'I'm desperate to try out my new stopwatch,' said Milo.

'And it's more fun in the snow, even though you can't go so fast,' said Mia.

'I love the snow!' said Birdy. 'It's totally awesome.'

'All right then. Try not to fall over!' said Mum. She was in a very good mood because Dad had given her a lovely silver locket. She was wearing it round her neck and kept playing with it. Dad was very jolly too, because Mum had given him the special jacket with all the secret pockets he'd been wanting for ages. He was wearing it now, even though it was really warm in the kitchen.

The children put on all their hats and coats and scarves and gloves and wellington boots. Birdy was in such a hurry, she put her left boot on her right foot and her right boot on her left and wondered why walking was suddenly so difficult. Mia sorted her out, and they ran through the back door, grabbing their bag of chocolates on the way.

They had a couple of races along the lane so they could honestly say that was what they'd done to Mum and Dad. They weren't real races. Milo held Birdy with one hand and Mia held Birdy with the

other and all three of them galloped along together and ended joint first. Then Mia timed Milo with his new stopwatch while Birdy hopped about making patterns in the snow. His speed was very impressive, even when hampered by his boots.

'Now I'll time you, Mia,' he said.

She ran as fast as she could, but she staggered once or twice and knew Milo must have run much faster than her.

'Well? How did I do?' she said breathlessly.

'Wow! You've beaten me by one second!' said Milo.

'Never!' said Mia.

'Truly,' said Milo, showing her the watch. He *might* just have pressed it five seconds after she'd started, because he'd seen her tiny not-really-a-present under the Christmas tree and felt sorry for her. Or maybe Mia really did run faster. It made her happy anyway, and the stones in her stomach eased a little.

They jumped over the ditch, walked right into the Enchanted Wood ... and stopped in awe. Birdy was so taken aback, she didn't even manage to say 'awesome', though it certainly was. All the trees were decorated with silver tinsel and glass baubles every colour of the rainbow and tiny silver bells. The squirrels and rabbits all wore little scarlet Christmas jumpers, some patterned with stars, some with snowflakes. They scampered in the snow, the squirrels sometimes darting up the decorated trees, the rabbits merrily rolling in the snow.

They paused to chatter, 'Happy Christmas,' to

the children, and Milo, Mia and Birdy chorused it back. The birds flying above them sang it loud and clear and the children sang it back to them. The trees waved their branches so that snow drifted down and the silver bells rang out, plainly saying, 'Happy Christmas,' too.

Milo and Mia and Birdy darted in and out of the trees until they reached the wonderful Magic Faraway Tree. It was twinkling with fairy lights, and silver and gold medallions hung from every branch. Milo plucked one from the tree and started peeling the silver paper excitedly.

'They're chocolate!' he said and popped it in his mouth. 'White chocolate – my favourite. Oh, yum, yum, yum!' he mumbled, his mouth full. He accidentally dropped the silver wrapper – but instead of falling in the snow it grew wings and flew up to a branch, settling as a beautiful butterfly decoration.

Mia plucked a gold medallion and unpeeled the gold paper. As she bit into the lovely smooth milk chocolate the gold paper sprang out of her hand and flew upwards too, a tiny golden bird.

'Oh, I want to make a bird too, because I'm Birdy!' Birdy said and jumped up to snatch a really big gold medallion. She scrabbled at the edge of the gold wrapping, finding it difficult because she had rather bitten nails, but managed to get it off the chocolate by sheer determination. The gold paper spiralled into the air, whirled round her head twice and then flew up on to a snowy branch, perching there decoratively.

'Oh, ow lubbly!' said Birdy indistinctly, her mouth full of chocolate. She reached for another medallion.

'Don't try to eat them all, Birdy!' said Milo. 'There won't be any left for anyone else.'

'There isn't anyone else around,' said Birdy, plucking a silver medallion this time.

Just as she said that the trapdoor at the bottom of the tree sprang open and a small squirrel in a red snowflake jumper sitting on a cushion came whizzing out, squealing with delight.

'I've been down Moonface's slippery-slip all by myself!' he announced proudly. 'And I wasn't a bit scared.'

'Then you deserve a medal,' said Birdy, and she handed him her silver medallion.

He picked off the silver easily with his tiny claws and then squealed even louder as the paper flew into the air.

'Oh, dear, the tree's chocolate medallions are so lovely that our Christmas presents are going to seem very ordinary,' said Mia.

'Still, chocolate's chocolate,' said Milo. 'And I'm not even sure the Angry Pixie deserves his. Don't you remember how he kept chucking that vase of water over me last summer?'

'Yes, but he seems much nicer now he's made friends with the Saucepan Man and Mr Watzisname,' said Mia.

They climbed rapidly and soon reached the Angry Pixie's house. They knocked politely at his door, knowing how annoyed he got when anyone tapped on his window. He came to the door wearing a large white apron alarmingly splattered with crimson.

'Oh, Mr Pixie, have you cut yourself?' said Milo.

'No, no, dear chap – I'm making lingonberry

cordial for my dear friends up above,' the Angry Pixie said. 'They've invited me to Christmas dinner. The cordial is my little contribution to the festive meal. Would you like to try some?'

'Yes please!' said the children.

He brought them out three small glasses of the dark red juice. They wished him a happy Christmas and took big sips. Their mouths were still coated with sweet chocolate. The sharpness of the lingonberries came as a shock. The cordial was so sour that they sucked in their cheeks, struggling not to make faces.

'Delicious, isn't it?' said the Angry Pixie proudly.

'Yes, wonderful,' said Milo, not daring to suggest he should add some sugar to the mixture. He didn't want the pixie to pour a pitcher of cordial over his head.

'Would you like to have some more? I've got plenty,' said the Angry Pixie.

'No thank you, Mr Pixie, we have to be on our way. But here's a little Christmas present,' said Mia, and she handed him a bar of fudge chocolate.

The Angry Pixie went almost as red as his cordial, which was alarming – but it was simply because he was so pleased. He wished the children a happy Christmas all over again, and they wished he had a happy Christmas back, and then climbed further up the tree.

'I just can't wait to see Silky!' said Birdy.

'I can't wait to see her too,' said Milo. 'I hope she gives us some of her special hot chocolate. I'm still all shuddery after that sour pixie cordial.'

They knocked on Silky's yellow door. They waited a little and knocked again. Still no answer. The children looked at each other.

'Perhaps she's gone to wish Moonface a happy Christmas?' Mia suggested.

'Or nipped up to the top of the tree already to see what land's up there?' said Milo.

'Oh, I did want to see her *now*!' Birdy wailed – and at that moment the door flew open. There was Silky, still in her nightie, her lovely, long hair tangled around her shoulders, her wings drooping.

'Here I am, Birdy!' she said, giving her a big hug.

'Happy Christmas, all of you! I must have slept in! I'm so sorry! I've only been back an hour or so.'

'You've been riding around with Santa, haven't you?' said Birdy. 'Oh, it must have been such fun!'

'It was wonderful!' said Silky dreamily. 'We went so fast! And several times the children were still awake and we had to go back to them later on. And once a whole sack of presents tipped out of the sleigh, but Santa managed to direct the reindeer downwards fast enough to catch it before it tumbled on the ground.'

'He came to us!' said Birdy.

'I know, I know!' said Silky. 'And did you all like your presents?'

'We've had our stockings, but we're going to open our big presents after breakfast when we get back,' said Milo quickly.

The stones clanked in Mia's tummy again, but she managed to stay smiling.

'Shall we let you go back to sleep, Silky? You must be so tired,' she said.

'No, I'll give myself some of my wake-up cordial

and then I'll be fine,' she said. 'I'll give you all some too, though you seem wide awake already.'

'It's not that dark red cordial, is it?' said Milo warily. 'We've already had some from the Angry Pixie. And I don't really think we can manage any more!'

Silky took a big jug from her cupboard and four crystal glasses.

'I think you'll be able to manage a few sips of mine,' she said. She poured herself a glassful.

The children looked at it, trying not to wrinkle their noses rudely. It was a deep *green* colour and looked as if it was made from kale and cabbage and broccoli – all the vegetables they tried hard not to eat.

Silky took three great gulps of her cordial, draining her glass. Right before their eyes her nightdress turned into a shimmering silver fairy frock, her wings uncrumpled and her hair smoothed into long, shining waves.

Birdy's eyes grew big. 'Silky, will I turn into a fairy if I drink some of that green yucky stuff?' she asked hopefully.

'I don't think you can turn into an actual fairy, Birdy – but it will certainly make you feel great,' said Silky. 'Shall I pour you a glass?'

'Yes please,' said Birdy, holding her nose in readiness to choke it down without spluttering.

Silky poured the gloopy green liquid, but as it splashed into Birdy's glass it lost all colour and consistency and became the palest shade of pink, fizzing delightfully. Birdy took a tentative sip and then swallowed eagerly, gulping down half the glass without pausing.

'It's awesome!' she said, hiccupping. 'Kind of pink lemonady, but better, and so fizzy that it tickles!'

Silky poured Milo a glass. He watched carefully, his face close up so that he could actually sniff the sharp vegetable smell – and yet as the cordial hit his glass it paled into the smoothest creamiest vanilla, with little streaks of glistening gold. He took a great big gulp and then grinned, his lips smeared white.

'Wow! It's a bit like a salted caramel milkshake – utterly amazing,' he said, offering Mia a sip.

'I'll pour Mia her own glass,' said Silky.

'Maybe mine will stay all green and lumpy – just my luck,' Mia muttered.

'Let's see!' said Silky. She poured from the jug, and the mixture turned a beautiful yellow with just a blush of red, with a cloud of whipped white on top. Mia drank, and discovered it was an incredible sweet peachy juice swirled with cream. She swallowed and felt the magic juice slide down her throat, soothing and delicious.

'Oh, Silky! Mine's the best!' Mia said.

They offered Silky her bar of chocolate, again a little embarrassed because it felt so ordinary, but she seemed delighted.

'I've never had a real chocolate bar before!' she said. 'This is almost too special to eat!'

Even so, Silky unwrapped it carefully and took one small square of white chocolate.

'Oh, it's wonderful – so much better than all my homemade stuff!' she said.

The children disagreed with her heartily, but were very pleased she liked it so.

'We've got Moonface some chocolate too!' said Birdy.

'Let's go and wish him a happy Christmas,' said Silky. 'I hope he hasn't slept in like me. He was up till very late last night wrapping special little nut parcels for all his squirrel friends.'

'I think he must be up, because we saw a little squirrel having a ride on the slippery-slip,' said Mia.

When they climbed up to Moonface's house they could hardly get near his door for squirrels queuing up, chattering and laughing and jumping

about. Silky gently pushed past them, the children following, and they squeezed inside. Moonface's round little room was teeming with squirrels, all of them clutching their nut parcels and circling the slippery-slip eagerly.

'Now then, chaps, calm down! You have to slide one at a time or else you'll all get stuck! Come along now – form an orderly queue,' said Moonface, rushing round in a tizz.

'Shall we form an orderly queue too?' Silky asked.

Moonface looked up and beamed. 'Silky! And Milo, Mia and Birdy! Happy Christmas, my dears! Do come and help me dispatch these dear little fellows down the slippery-slip and then we can have a proper Christmas hug.'

It was quite a task. The squirrels were never very obedient at the best of times, and today they were so overexcited they found it impossible to keep still. They dashed this way and that, waving their tails wildly in the air, so at least Moonface's furniture got a good dusting. Even Silky couldn't organise them, so they just had to wait patiently until the last little squeaking squirrel disappeared down the slippery-slip, shrieking with excitement.

Then Moonface sat down, mopping his large white forehead, exhausted.

'Happy Christmas, dearest friends,' he murmured weakly. 'You must let me make you a cup of tea.'

In actual fact Silky boiled his kettle, Milo fetched the cups and saucers, Mia spooned tea into the fat brown teapot and Birdy fetched the sugar lumps (and helped herself to one secretly). They let Moonface graciously do the actual pouring of the tea.

'You must try one of my biscuits too – a brand-new recipe!' he said. 'Could you possibly fetch the biscuit tin for me, little Birdy?'

She did as she was asked and prised the lid open. The golden biscuits inside the tin were drizzled with a yellow sauce, and smelt delicious.

'Mmm! What sort of biscuits are they, Moonface?' she asked, handing the tin round to everyone.

'Sherbet Surprise,' Moonface said proudly. 'Take a big bite, everyone!'

Silky just took a nibble. Milo and Mia each took

a very large bite. Birdy crammed her entire biscuit into her mouth. The biscuit was crisp at first, but became softer as they chewed. It tasted deliciously lemony and became weirdly fizzy. Then, just like Moonface's Toffee Shocks, the biscuit grew and grew the more they chewed, making speech impossible.

'Ouble ouble ouble!' said Milo, dribbling.

'Ouble!' Mia agreed, trying to swallow.

'OUBLE!' Birdy gasped, her eyes wide. Then, just as she thought she would have to forget her manners and spit the biscuit right out, it suddenly burst with such a big bubbly fizz that she had a coughing fit.

Mia thumped Birdy on the back, her eyes watering as her own biscuit exploded.

'These are the greatest biscuits ever!' said Milo, roaring with laughter.

'Can I have another?' Birdy gasped.

'Maybe not just yet,' said Silky wisely.

'They're great, aren't they?' said Moonface happily. 'I don't want to boast, but I do feel I'm good at inventing new recipes. I think my Sherbet Surprises are right up there with Toffee Shocks, don't you?'

They all agreed with him – and when they were ready for another cup of tea they all indulged in another biscuit, though Birdy didn't try to eat hers in one go this time.

'I'll take one up to young Pippin. I think he'll like them too,' said Moonface.

'Let us give you our Christmas present first, Moonface,' said Mia shyly, and handed him a bar of toffee chocolate.

'I'm afraid it's ordinary toffee, and it doesn't give you a shock, but it still tastes quite nice,' Milo explained.

Moonface took a bite and declared it was more than quite nice – it was utterly delicious. He took another bite and then another, and in less than a minute the wrapper was empty and the contents were all in Moonface's tummy. He patted it happily.

'Thank you so much, my dears! Much appreciated! Now, let's pop up the tree!'

They looked in on Dame Washalot and her friend

Dame Ironallday as they went. There was no danger of getting drenched in Dame Washalot's discarded water from her washing tub. The dames had a special Christmas holiday like everyone else. They weren't wearing their usual mob caps and pinafores and work dresses with rolled up sleeves. They wore their best frocks, Dame Washalot in green velvet and Dame Ironallday in a complementary shade of purple, with matching necklaces of jade and amethyst beads. They had their best patent heeled shoes lined up ready to slip on, but still wore their fluffy slippers for comfort in the house.

'Happy Christmas, dames!' everyone said.

'Happy Christmas to you, Silky and Moonface!' said Dame Washalot.

'Happy Christmas to you, children!' said Dame Ironallday.

'We should have renamed ourselves yesterday. We were both Dame Bakealotalldaylong! Would you like to try a Christmas cookie each?' said Dame Washalot, fetching a tin.

They'd been baking little cinnamon cookies,

which tasted delicious, though they smelt very faintly of soapy water and hot ironing. The children ate them gingerly, waiting for them to change flavour or explode, but the dames weren't magical like Silky and Moonface, so there were no shocks or surprises.

'We've brought you a little present too,' said Mia, giving them a chocolate coconut bar. Luckily there were two sections under the wrapping paper so the dames could have one each.

'Oh, coconut, what a lovely flavour!' said Dame Washalot.

'Oh, chocolate too, sheer heaven!' said Dame Ironallday.

'Are you going up the tree to see little Pippin?' asked Dame Washalot.

'Perhaps the dear chap would like a cinnamon cookie for his breakfast?' asked Dame Ironallday, and she parcelled several cookies up in tissue paper and gave them to Mia to pass on to him.

They all wished each other a happy Christmas again, and then Silky and Moonface and Milo and

Mia and Birdy climbed further up the tree.

They found Pippin curled up in his cosy bear cave, fast asleep and sucking his paw.

'Happy Christmas, little Pippin!' Silky said softly, giving him a kiss.

Pippin opened his eyes and then gave a little shriek of excitement.

'Happy Christmas!' he cried, wrapping his paws round Silky in a proper bear hug. He bounced about in his blue flannel pyjamas (Silky had made him a special pair to keep him warm in the winter) and gave everyone a big hug.

'What's this, Pippin?' said Moonface, pointing to the end of the bed. He'd lent Pippin one of his long stripy socks to hang up – and now it was looking very fat and lumpy!

'Did Santa really come!' Pippin said, clapping his paws.

'Better have a look and see!' said Moonface.

It was very dark in Pippin's cave, so Silky lit a candle. Pippin's face glowed in the flickering light, his eyes very big and round as he delved in the sock.

He found a tiny wooden bear toy, a penny whistle, a yo-yo, a bag of marbles and a pot of honey. There was a wrapped present too. Pippin pummelled it eagerly with his paws and he heard a tiny squeak. He tore the paper off – and there was a golden teddy bear holding out his arms.

'Oh, a teddy to be my special friend!' Pippin cried, hugging him. 'I'm so lucky! I shall call him . . . Hugabug! Do you like that name, Hugabug?' he asked, and made the teddy nod emphatically.

'You must have been a very good little bear for Santa to bring you so many lovely presents,' said Silky.

Mia found herself clutching her stomach. She'd been a good child, hadn't she? Well, reasonably so. She was sure she'd been just as good as Milo or Birdy. Still, it was no use brooding about it.

'We've brought you a small present too, Pippin,' she said, handing him a honeycomb crunch bar.

Pippin bit into it at once, without waiting to take off the wrapper.

'Hey, hey, you don't eat the paper!' said Milo, helping him.

Pippin pretended to feed Hugabug – but all his mouthfuls ended up inside Pippin!

'It's yummy, yummy, yummy!' he said, grinning with chocolatey teeth.

'You'd better clean those teeth now and have a quick wash and pull on your warmest jumper and your duffle coat,' said Silky. 'We're going up to the top of the tree to wish the Saucepan Man and Mr Watzisname a happy Christmas.'

'And then we'll be bobbing our heads through the clouds to see which magic land has arrived,' said Moonface. 'I think I've guessed!'

'Sh, Moonface, let it be a surprise for Pippin and the children,' said Silky.

Pippin was ready in a flash (though Silky had to give his face and paws another good wipe after he'd washed) and then the six of them (seven if you counted Hugabug) climbed up to the Saucepan Man's home at the top. He and his dear friend Mr Watzisname were wearing white tunics and blue checked trousers and floppy chef hats. They were charging around the kitchen, stuffing a very

big turkey and preparing lots of vegetables.

'Two men busy cooking,
Two ladies for dinner.
Both are so charming,
We're on to a winner!'

the Saucepan Man sang cheekily, while Mr Watzisname tapped in time to the song on a spare kettle.

'Have you invited Dame Washalot and Dame Ironallday for Christmas dinner?' said Silky, giggling. 'No wonder they were all dressed up in their finest clothes!'

'We're making a special pudding for them too!' said the Saucepan Man, glancing at a pot already bubbling on the stove. 'I'm steaming a suet pudding, with lots of golden syrup. Mr Watzisname's in charge of the custard.'

'Though I did wonder if the dames might prefer a chocolate dessert,' said Mr Watzisname. 'I've heard ladies are very partial to chocolate.' He looked at

Silky and Mia and Birdy for confirmation.

'Steam puddings are lovely too,' said Silky tactfully.

'And you can share this little Christmas present with them after you've eaten your syrup pudding,' said Mia, and she handed them each a bar of flaky chocolate.

They were utterly delighted and insisted on giving everyone a spoonful of their golden syrup in return. It was too sweet for Silky, so Pippin licked up her spoonful very happily too.

'Is the Angry Pixie coming to dinner with you as well?' Milo asked.

'He'd be very welcome, but he has a prior engagement, up there!' said the Saucepan Man, pointing upwards.

'In the magic land? Do you know which land it is?' Mia asked eagerly.

'Can't you guess?' said Mr Watzisname. 'We were up there making merry at the crack of dawn!'

'I know what it is!' said Birdy, jumping up and down. 'It's the Land of Christmas!'

CHAPTER
FOURTEEN

BIRDY SCRAMBLED up the ladder with Mia and Milo and Silky and Moonface. They stood still, holding hands. It was indeed the Land of Christmas. There was crisp snow everywhere, but the sun was shining brightly and the sky was bright blue. Robins flew above their heads, chirping merrily. Folk danced along the streets wearing velvet cloaks and fancy hats, wishing each other a merry Christmas. Carol singers gathered on every corner, singing their hearts out. Church bells rang and sleigh bells tinkled and street sellers cried their wares: roasted chestnuts, mulled wine, mince pies, candy canes!

'It's just like one of those lovely old-fashioned Christmas cards!' said Mia. 'I wonder if we can have a sleigh ride?'

She ran to where a sleigh was waiting, four splendid white horses in harness breathing down their nostrils in the frosty air. An elf in a smart green suit smiled at her cheerily as Mia patted the horses.

'Of course you and your friends can have a ride. That's what we're here for. Jump in!'

The sleigh was wonderfully comfortable, with red upholstered seats, lots of squashy cushions and big woolly rugs to keep everyone warm. They piled in – the children in the front and Silky and Moonface in the back. Silky had Pippin on her lap to keep him safe, and he had Hugabug on his lap to keep *him* safe. The elf flipped the reins and the horses set off, the harness bells jingling.

They went slowly through the crowded snowy streets, but soon they were out in the countryside and could speed along.

'Wheeeee!' said Birdy, having to hang on tight to her bobble hat. 'This is totally awesome!'

'Was it as good as this in Santa's sleigh?' Mia asked Silky.

'This is much more comfortable,' said Silky. 'It was wonderful flying through the air with Santa, but on the outward journeys it was a terrible squash with all the presents piled high.'

'Still, it must have been fantastic to actually fly,' said Milo.

'Mmm,' said Silky thoughtfully. 'Moonface dear, do you remember any flying spells?'

'Oh, Silky – it was so long ago, and I was not very good at spell-learning. But hang on, I seem to dimly remember . . . How did it go?

'*Waggle your ears and cross one eye.*
Clasp your thumbs and slap one thigh.
Hold your breath and try and try . . .
And you will fly!'

Moonface declared triumphantly.

Then he rose up in the air, shrieking and waggling his legs, trying hard to get back in the sleigh.

Silky just managed to grab Moonface by one ankle, while Milo reached out precariously and caught the other leg, and between them they stuffed him back in the sleigh.

'We want *all* of us to fly, Moonface, not just you!' said Silky, patting him on the back to help him recover. 'Shall we try again, together? I think my own magic powers are still working!'

They chanted their way through the spell and changed the last line to '*And we will* all *fly, sleigh and horses too, right up to the sky!*' The horses gathered speed, their hooves ringing on the frosty road. The runners on the sleigh slid so fast that sparks flew. They clutched each other as the sleigh shook violently, and the elf driver juggled the reins, struggling to keep control.

Then they were suddenly *up*, just a fraction at first, but truly in the air, and then they went higher, smoothly now, almost without effort. The horses galloped over treetops, over roofs, over steeples, while the children screamed in surprise and delight – even Milo, who had no head for heights. Pippin was used to climbing to the tops of trees, but when he peeped over the side of the sleigh he was so unnerved he shut his eyes tight and clutched Silky. Luckily he remembered to hang on tight to Hugabug. Silky was used to flying, of course, and had already had an airborne sleigh ride with Santa, so she was perfectly relaxed. But poor Moonface quivered all over, his large white face going pale green.

'Are you all right, Moonface?' Silky shouted in his ear, because the whistling wind was so noisy.

'No!' Moonface quavered. 'I am very much all wrong! I don't like it one bit. I feel horribly wibbly-wobbly! I want to go *down*!'

'Then say the spell for going down, Moonface dear! I hate to see you in such a state,' said Silky.

'But I don't know one!' Moonface admitted, struggling not to burst into tears. 'I don't think I bothered to listen when we had that lesson at Enchanter School. So now we're condemned to be stuck up in the air for ever, and very soon I will disgrace myself by being sick!'

'No you won't! I will get us down again, I

promise,' said Silky, holding his clammy hand.

She tried willing the sleigh to go down, making so much effort that her head throbbed, but she wasn't quite magic enough to manage it, though the horses faltered and the sleigh bobbed about alarmingly. Moonface moaned, but Silky squeezed his hand.

'I will make up my own spell!' she said determinedly. She took a deep breath and then said,

'Please let us descend
At a reasonable speed,
For the sake of my friend,
Who is in dire need!'

The elf called a command to the horses, and they gradually slowed to a stately trot through thin air, their heads lowered so that they went gently down and down and down. The sleigh followed smoothly, and within minutes they were gliding along the road again. Moonface thanked Silky fervently, mopping his face, thankful that the children in front hadn't even noticed his distress.

The elf adjusted his cap, which had been blown sideways by the wind, and took a deep breath.

'Well! That was an interesting experience!' he murmured to himself, and his horses snorted to each other, saying much the same.

The sleigh drew up beside a frozen lake where many people were skating.

'Oh, please can we skate too!' said Milo. 'I love skating!'

'Fantastic!' said Mia. 'I know I can skate better than you, Milo!'

'Awesome!' said Birdy. 'I bet I'm better than *both* of you!'

In actual fact the best ice-skater was Pippin! The elf at the boot booth had a little trouble kitting him out with boots because his paws were a different shape to the average foot, but he managed to find a perfect pair of scarlet boots that fitted Pippin perfectly.

'Oh, wow! Look at my red boots!' said Pippin, staggering across the snowy grass to the edge of the lake.

'Wait, Pippin! Don't you want to hold my hand?' said Silky, hurriedly tying the laces of her own white boots.

But as soon as Pippin stepped on to the frozen lake, he stood up straight and then glided in smooth strokes across the ice, holding his head up, his arms out, his legs strong and steady. Then he started racing round, faster than anyone else, whooping with glee, red boots flashing.

'Slow down, Pippin! You'll knock someone over!' Silky shouted.

Pippin took no notice, enjoying showing off. He experimented with little jumps, and then stood on one skate and whirled round and round so cleverly that the people on the ice laughed and clapped him.

'I bet we can do that too, eh, Mia?' said Milo, dashing forward – and promptly falling over.

'Watch me!' said Mia, but she staggered, lost her balance and fell too.

Silky hung on to Birdy and steered her round until she grew confident.

'Look at me – I'm skating!' she shouted, rosy-cheeked with triumph.

Silky was inevitably graceful, but her spread wings helped her balance, otherwise she might have fallen over too. Moonface sat on a bench at the side of the lake, just happy to be back on firm ground again, but when he'd recovered he hired himself a fine pair of shiny black boots and found he rather liked skating. He went round at a slow stately pace, his face a healthy bright white again.

Milo and Mia began to get the hang of skating, and soon managed to swoop across the ice without staggering, loving every minute. Then everyone formed a long line – Pippin and Hugabug at the front, then Birdy, then Silky, then Milo, then Mia, then Moonface at the back – and they skated together, snaking this way and that, while a little elf band played 'The Skater's Waltz'.

There were food and drink stalls under the trees, so they decided to have a little snack because they were all starving hungry from the exercise. They gave their boots back at the booth. Pippin took his off obediently, but clutched them to his chest, looking woebegone.

'We don't have many bear customers, so you might as well keep them, little chap,' said the kindly elf behind the counter. 'Happy Christmas!'

'Happy Christmas and thank you, thank you, thank you!' said Pippin, dancing with joy. He popped Hugabug into one of the boots for safety.

They all had little bowls of cheesy chips and hot apple juice. Pippin was hugging his boots as if he could never let them go, so Silky had to feed him and hold his mug of juice to his lips. Mia helped the sleigh driver give the horses their nosebags and they munched happily too.

When everyone felt refreshed they hopped back into the sleigh and were taken towards the hills in the distance. There were lots of birds flying above them – not just robins with their red breasts, but Milo spotted a partridge, Silky saw two turtle doves and Birdy saw three hens pecking in the snowy grass. Four blackbirds sang a sweet song, which Mia tried to imitate.

'It's as if they're calling to me!' she said, and then suddenly burst out laughing. 'Four calling birds! It's that Christmas song, "The Twelve Days of Christmas". We sing it at school!'

'So what comes next?' said the sleigh elf, smiling. 'Could it possibly be five gold rings?'

He produced five golden rings from his pocket and gave one to Silky, one to Moonface and one to each of the children. They were only gold paper, but they still looked splendid. Pippin couldn't wear rings because he didn't have fingers – and he didn't mind a jot anyway, because he was so happy to have Hugabug and his splendid scarlet boots.

The elf slowed the horses to a gentle walking pace so they could all spot the six geese squawking as they laid their eggs and the seven swans trying to swim in the icy stream and eight maids milking the brown cows in a barn. The elf stopped the horses altogether when they came to a little village square where nine fine ladies were picking up their skirts and dancing and ten red-faced lords were leaping wildly while eleven pipers played a merry tune and twelve bandsmen beat their drums.

The children and Pippin and Silky and Moonface all jumped out of the sleigh and danced and leapt too, while the elf watched, clapping them. Then they piled back in again, so warm now they didn't need to huddle under the blankets. The sleigh took them nearer the hills. They were dotted with little people hurtling down the hills on sledges. A few pixie children were on the lower slopes, sliding on tea trays.

'Can we have a go?' Milo and Mia asked their driver eagerly.

'Can I?' said Birdy. 'I could have a tea tray if a sledge is too big for me.'

'I definitely want a sledge,' said Milo.

'So do I!' said Mia.

Milo and Mia were trusted with a sledge each from the shelter at the bottom of the hill. Birdy shared a sledge with Moonface and Pippin squashed up with Silky on her sledge, insisting on taking his boots and Hugabug for a ride too.

'What about you, Mr Elf?' Milo said. 'Wouldn't you like to sledge?'

'I had fun sledging when I was a little elflet, but I'm happy to stay with my horses and read my paper nowadays,' said the elf. 'It's the special Christmas edition. Well, it always is!'

It was a long trudge up the hill with the sleighs, but it proved worth it when they got to the top and had a splendid view over the hills and valleys and villages of the Land of Christmas. Then they clambered on to their sledges, took a deep breath, and pushed off.

'Wheeeeeee!' yelled Milo.

'Wheeeeeee!' yelled Mia.

'Wheeeeeee!' yelled Birdy and Moonface.

'Wheeeeeee!' yelled Pippin and Silky.

It was just like flying. Silky even wondered if it was *better* than flying! They hurtled downwards, almost colliding, but somehow staying on course, on and on and on until they eventually reached the bottom of the slope.

'That was the best thing *ever*!' said Milo.

'Can we go again?' said Mia.

'Let's beat them this time, Moonface!' said Birdy.

'No, we'll come first, won't we, Silky?' said Pippin.

They had so many goes that they *all* had a turn at finishing first. They were starting to get hungry all over again when they heard bells clanging far away in the distance.

'Oh, my, I think it's nearly Christmas dinnertime!' said Moonface.

'Jump in and I'll take you to the feasting site,' said the elf. He patted his tummy. 'I'm meeting up with all my own elfin folk.'

'I can't wait to see my fairy sisters!' said Silky, her face glowing.

'I've heard word I'm an uncle now!' said Moonface. 'I'm longing to see the little Moon-baby! My dear old mum is *over* the moon to be a granny at last!'

'Will I see my bear mother?' Pippin asked hopefully.

Silky gave him a hug. 'I don't think bears come to the Land of Christmas for their special family festive dinner. But never mind. You're my own adopted fairy bear so you can come with us. My sisters will think you're such a poppet. They'll all wish they had a little bear too.'

The children looked at each other as they climbed into the sleigh.

'What about us?' said Milo.

'You're our best friends,' said Moonface. 'You're practically family.'

'Does that mean we're like fairies and pixies?' Birdy asked excitedly. 'Awesome!'

Milo and Mia looked uncertain. They weren't very sure they wanted to be token fairies or even pixies. But they were fascinated when the sleigh whizzed them all the way back to the village at the top of the ladder and they saw the preparation for the family feast.

Huge white open-sided marquees had been erected on the nearby fields, with flaming torches all around to keep everyone warm. They were already crowded with fairy folk and pixies and elves, all laughing and greeting each other and choosing tables, which were set with plates and cutlery and glasses and Christmas crackers. At both ends, huge long tables were piled with food – golden basted

turkeys and pink hams and little sausages and nut roasts and crispy roast potatoes and soft white mashed potatoes and all kinds of vegetables and Christmas puddings and yellow custard and red and green jelly and fruit pies and all different flavours of ice cream.

The children stared in astonishment, speechless. Birdy couldn't even manage an 'awesome'.

'How...?' gasped Milo, meaning how had the marquees been erected so quickly and where had all the food come from and how did the turkey stay hot and yet the ice cream cold and how did everyone find their families in this huge crowd?

Silky and Moonface said, 'As if by magic!' and smiled.

'Silky! Oh, Silky!' A fairy came running over, almost Silky's twin, with very long hair and beautiful clothes and shimmering wings, and then another and another and another, and the five lovely fairies danced round in a family hug, with Pippin squashed between them, clutching his red boots and Hugabug protectively. They all exclaimed over Pippin and tickled him under the chin and said he was the cutest little bear ever.

'Moonface, my boy!' A small old lady with a very large, pale face came running along, very spry for her age, and threw her arms round him, giving him great smacking kisses on both cheeks.

'Oh, Mum!' said Moonface bashfully, kissing her back.

A big crowd of Moonface's family surrounded him, including his proud sister holding a dear little baby, who was the spitting image of her uncle. Moonface took her in his arms and she gurgled happily, pinching his nose and kicking her chubby legs.

Another group of pixies were having a much noisier reunion, greeting each other excitedly, but almost immediately quarrelling over which table to sit at, and arguing who was the eldest and most important. Even the little pixlets were squabbling, pulling each other's big, pointy ears. One of the gentlemen pixies was admonishing them crossly. He was holding a large pitcher of some dark liquid and was threatening to pour it over their heads if they didn't calm down.

'It's the Angry Pixie!' Milo exclaimed.

'Oh, I do hope he doesn't throw that juice all over them! It'll stain their party outfits horribly,' said Mia.

'But it will look funny!' said Milo.

'No, it will be horrid!' said Birdy, who hated it when anyone quarrelled.

But the Angry Pixie managed to keep his temper and pour his crimson juice into the glasses on the table. They heard him say, 'Happy Christmas, everyone!' and he raised his glass. They all raised their glasses too, even the littlest pixlet.

'Oh, dear, I bet they spit it out!' said Milo.

But Silky was watching too and realised what was likely to happen. She stared at the juice, waving her fingers. Sprinkles of sugar fell into each glass and sparkled there.

'Silky's sweetening it!' said Birdy. 'She's so magic! Oh, I wish, wish, wish I was a fairy!'

'Come and join us at our table!' Silky called – but

already there was a whole crowd of fairy folk gathering around her, from baby fairy buds to magnificent ancient fairies with long silver hair and wise faces.

'Come and sit with us!' Moonface called, dandling his new little niece on his knee, but all the Moon relations took up so much room that there wasn't a single chair free.

The Angry Pixies were· beckoning too, smacking their crimson lips happily, their mood wondrously sweetened, but the children sensed that another quarrel might start any minute.

'Do you know what?' said Milo. 'Shall we go home to *our* family now?'

'Yes, let's,' said Mia. 'We've got our own Christmas dinner to eat at home.'

'And we've still got our big presents to open!' said Birdy.

Mia clutched her tummy, but said bravely, 'Yes, let's see what we've got!'

They waved goodbye to Silky and Moonface and the Angry Pixie and promised that they'd come back tomorrow. The elves were all at their own huge tables, relaxing after their hard work, but the sleigh elf jumped up and offered to escort them to the ladder down through the clouds to the Magic Faraway Tree.

'No, please just enjoy yourself with your family,' said Mia.

'Thank you so much for taking us everywhere,' said Milo. He looked across the tables and saw all the elves they'd met during their visits to the Land of Sunshine and the Land of Toys. 'Thank you, everyone!' he shouted, and they all waved back and called, 'Happy Christmas!'

'We won't get lost, will we?' said Birdy, holding hands with Milo and Mia.

'No, we'll find the ladder easy-peasy, you'll see,' said Mia.

It was surprisingly easy actually because some helpful elf had scrawled 'Ladder!' with a pointing arrow in the snow. They climbed down in a trice, through the clouds, and paused on their way down the tree to peer through the Saucepan Man's little latticed window. He was wearing his best suit and a spotted bow tie, with just two of his shiniest kettles slung on a string round his neck so he could still clank as he walked. Mr Watzisname was even more formally dressed in a dinner jacket with a white tie, but he'd obviously mislaid the matching trousers so wore his usual corduroys, tied at the baggy knees with festive ribbon instead of old string.

The two dames were there already, sitting together on the sofa, their cheeks and lips unnaturally bright with make-up. They held sherry glasses in their hands, sipped daintily and tittered whenever the Saucepan Man or Mr Watzisname made a joke. A delicious smell of cooking dinner drifted out of the slightly open window.

'Mmm! I'm getting really hungry!' said Milo.

'Yes, but remember it won't be lunchtime yet when we get home,' said Mia.

'Still, we get to eat chocolates on Christmas morning,' said Birdy, as they continued the long climb down the tree. 'Oh, we're so lucky! We get to have *two* Christmases! And I can't wait to open my Christmas presents! I've got so many!'

'Shut up, Birdy,' said Milo gently, nodding at Mia.

'Oh!' said Birdy. She tugged at her sister's scarf. 'I've got *too* many. You can have half of my presents, Mia.'

'And I'll share mine, whatever it is,' said Milo.

'Don't be silly,' said Mia briskly, though she was so touched she nearly burst into tears. 'You must both keep your presents. Don't worry about me. I expect I've got an extra-lovely Christmas card.'

She tried telling herself that all the way down the tree. They couldn't take their usual shortcut down Moonface's slippery-slip because he was up above the clouds. They helped themselves to chocolate medallions, which perked them up a little, but they were really tired when they got back down to the snowy grass at the bottom of the Faraway Tree. The sun was out now, but there was quite a strong breeze that blew the decorated branches of all the trees in the Enchanted Wood. They made a soft tinkling sound. *Wisha-wisha-wisha!*

'Oh, the trees are talking to us again!' said Birdy. She took a deep breath. 'We wish you a merry Christmas, trees!' she sang, and Milo and Mia joined in.

They went on singing all the way back, the trees helpfully pointing the way. Then they jumped over the ditch.

'Race you back to the cottage!' said Milo. He winked at Mia and she took the hint.

They both ran very slowly, almost jogging on the spot, while Birdy charged forward as fast as she could, her arms pumping, her feet sliding this way and that in her clumsy wellington boots.

'I won! I won! I won!' she shrieked triumphantly when she reached the gate, and Milo and Mia high-fived each other, grinning.

Mum and Dad had been busy in the kitchen and seemed to have all the preparations under control.

'Did you enjoy your racing, darlings?' Mum said, helping Birdy take off her winter coat and unwinding all her scarves.

'You've certainly got lovely rosy cheeks, all of you,' said Dad. 'I hope you're not too freezing. Hot chocolate, everyone?'

'Shall we have our presents first?' said Mia,

suddenly desperate to get the ordeal over.

So they went into the living room to the Christmas tree. Milo picked up his very big package and the smaller one. Birdy scampered about picking up her five parcels – one big one, one medium-sized and three little ones. Mia took hold of her one small, flat present and forced herself to smile. They sat down cross-legged, with Mum and Dad in the armchairs, watching eagerly.

'Shall I go first, seeing as I'm the oldest?' said Milo, already starting to tear at the wrapping paper, unable to help himself. Then he gave a great scream of utter joy. It was a games console! He had been longing for one for so long and now here it was! It had a game to go with it – *Dragonflame*, the game he'd been playing so intently in the Land of Toys.

'Wicked! Oh, thank you, thank you, thank you!' Milo yelled, giving Mum and Dad a hug.

'Thank Santa, not us,' said Mum.

'He knows just what a boy like you would want,' said Dad, grinning. 'And a dad like me too!

Now you open your present, Mia.'

Mia was having a struggle to keep a smile on her face, even though she was genuinely thrilled for Milo. She wasn't sure she was quite in control just yet.

'Birdy, you go next, as you're the youngest,' Mia said.

'OK!' said Birdy eagerly. She scrabbled with the biggest parcel. A turquoise ear poked out.

'Oh!' Birdy cried. 'Just a minute!' She ran upstairs and grabbed Gilbert, who was still having a doze on her bed. 'Gilbert, come and see! You might have a brother to play with!'

She dragged Gilbert down the stairs and sat him beside her. She opened the parcel right up . . . and Albert bounced out, grinning. Birdy gave him a big kiss and made Gilbert kiss him too. Then she started opening the first little parcel. It wasn't socks. It was a tiny furry turquoise puppy with floppy ears and big eyes. Birdy gasped in delight.

'AWESOME!' she cried, and grappled to get the wrapping paper off the other two parcels.

She discovered two more turquoise puppies, equally adorable.

'I love them! All of them! Gilbert and Albert can be the two daddies and these lovely little puppies can be their babies. What shall I call them?' She looked at Gilbert and Albert, but they didn't seem to know.

'How about Herbert?' said Mum.

'And . . . Egbert?' Dad suggested.

'There's a boy called Robert at school, but I don't like him much,' said Milo.

'I think the last little puppy is a girl,' said Mia. 'She can be Baby Berta.' She wished she was still young enough to believe that toy dogs were real. But no matter how she tried they just stayed sweet little toys – very cute, but not actually alive.

Still, Birdy made them jump about and tumble together in a very convincing way. Gilbert seemed startled to have acquired a whole new family so suddenly, but Birdy gave him a big hug and whispered in his ear that he was still her favourite, which cheered him up a lot.

'These are the best Christmas presents ever!' said Birdy, trying to hug all her dogs at the same time.

'You've got one more present to open still, Birdy!' said Dad.

'If it's another puppy, it's got very squashed,' said Milo, as Birdy took hold of the medium-sized flat parcel.

It wasn't a puppy at all. It was a fairy outfit – a silver sparkly dress just like Silky's – with silvery wings attached to the satin bodice, and silver ballet shoes in Birdy's exact size. She nearly fainted with joy and insisted on dressing up in it right that minute. The fairy outfit looked a little odd over her winter vest and thick knickers, but Birdy didn't care. She ran around, hoping she looked graceful, waving her fingers in the air as if she were making magic.

Mia wondered about asking Birdy to magic her own present into something exciting, just as a joke, but thought it might sound a bit sour.

'Now it's your turn, darling,' said Mum.

'Our special middle child,' said Dad.

Mia took a deep breath and opened up her small flat parcel. It was a card, though a lovely one – a photo of an adorable grey kitten with a white star-shaped patch on its face and little white socks on its paws.

'It's lovely!' Mia said shakily.

'Is that all?' said Milo.

'No, I think something might be inside,' said Mum.

Mia opened the card up. There was a voucher with gilt lettering. It said something about a riding stable at the top and there was Mia's name, and a promise of *six months'* worth of riding lessons!

'But . . . but riding lessons are so expensive!' she stammered, her hands trembling as she held the voucher.

'Santa has agreed a great deal with this riding stable back home. If you're prepared to act as a stable girl at weekends, they'll let you have lessons at a very reduced rate,' said Dad.

'You mean she's got to rake up all the horse muck?' said Milo, pulling a face.

'I don't mind a bit!' said Mia. 'I would *love* to be a stable girl because it's more time with the horses! Oh, how wonderful! This is an utterly magical present!'

She couldn't kiss the horses, so she kissed the photo of the kitten instead.

'Do you like that little kitten?' asked Mum. 'Does it say anything about it inside the card?'

Mia opened the card up again, still hanging on to her precious riding voucher. There was indeed a little message inside.

Hello! I'm Star! I live in a rescue home at the moment, but I'm nearly big enough to come and live with you. I will be able to be left when you go to school, but I do hope we'll have lots of cuddles and fun when you come home.

'Is this a message for *me*?' Mia whispered. 'I'm having riding lessons *and* my very own kitten!' She lost control altogether and big fat tears rolled down her cheeks.

'Oh, Mia, don't cry! Don't you like your presents? You can have one of my puppies if you want,' said Birdy.

'And you can play *Dragonflame* with me,' said Milo.

Mia stared at them. 'Thanks so much, but I'm crying because I couldn't truly be happier! I've got the best Christmas presents ever!'

'We all have!' said Milo.

'Can I sing my song now?' Birdy begged.

So they all sang 'We Wish You a Merry Christmas' many times, and truly no Christmas had ever been happier.

Meet our FARAWAY TREE FRIENDS

BIRDY is the youngest in the family and loves fairies, dressing up and her toy dog Gilbert.

MIA is the second eldest and is very fond of animals and drawing in her sketchbook. She hopes to be a vet one day.

MILO is the eldest sibling and loves running, playing video games and making things with wood.

MOONFACE lives at the very top. In his house is the start of the slippery-slip, a huge slide that curves all the way down inside the trunk of the tree.

SILKY lives below Moonface. She is the loveliest fairy you could ever imagine.

THE SAUCEPAN MAN is funny and he's great at making up songs. His saucepans make lots of noise when they jangle together.

Also available

an irresistible new story by bestselling author
Jacqueline Wilson.

Mia, Milo and Birdy are on a countryside holiday
when they discover the Enchanted Wood. Join their
adventures up the Magic Faraway Tree with
Moonface, Saucepan Man and Silky the fairy.

JACQUELINE WILSON

Jacqueline Wilson has been writing since she was 9 years old. She is one of Britain's bestselling and most beloved children's authors. The creator of Tracy Beaker, Hetty Feather and many other memorable characters, she has written more than 100 books and won numerous prizes. *The Magic Faraway Tree* was her favourite childhood story.

MARK BEECH

Mark Beech was born in Pendle, Lancashire, and loved to draw from an early age. His very popular work regularly includes scary dragons, wild dinosaurs, grumpy witches and many other wacky creatures. Mark lives in the Forest of Bowland.

Enid Blyton

is one of the most popular children's authors of all time. Her books have sold over 500 million copies and have been translated into other languages more often than any other children's author.

Enid Blyton adored writing for children. She wrote over 700 books and about 2,000 short stories. *The Famous Five* books, now 80 years old, are her most popular. She is also the author of other favourites including *The Secret Seven*, *The Magic Faraway Tree* and *Malory Towers*.

Born in London in 1897, Enid lived much of her life in Buckinghamshire and loved dogs, gardening and the countryside. She was very knowledgeable about trees, flowers, birds and animals.

Dorset – where some of the Famous Five's adventures are set – was a favourite place of hers too.

Enid Blyton's stories are read and loved by millions of children (and grown-ups) all over the world. Visit enidblyton.co.uk to discover more.

Illustration by
Laura Ellen Anderson.